Where Savanna Belongs

Book 1 of the Unexpected Inheritance Series

K.L.MacGrath

Copyright © Kimberly Oden

All rights reserved

The characters and events in this book are fictitious. Any similarity to real persons, living or dead, is coincidental and not intended by the author.

No part of this book may be reproduced or stored in a retrieval system, or transmitted in any form or by any means, electronic, mechanical, photocopying, recording, or otherwise without express written permission of the publisher.

Imprint: Independently published

Cover design by: Kimberly Oden
Printed in the United States of America

Dedication:

To the men and women in the military who write a blank check with their lives to defend and protect our country and serve with valor. And to my baby girl, Jaymie, who makes life worth living. And most of all to God. Much love and gratitude.

Success is not final, failure is not fatal: it is the courage to continue that counts.

Winston Churchill

~Chapter 1~

"*Thank God, I got Botox injections last month,*" Savanna St. James comforted herself as she paced the room in her black evening gown. Her long platinum-blonde hair was in a loose up-do to compliment her dress. Teeth whitened—check. Venetian bronzer fake tan—check. "*God, I know it's trivial, but please don't let me look orange tonight.*"

The sparkles from the diamond wreath around her neck danced in the light. The hideous scar from her left shoulder to her forearm was covered with a concealer.

Is it too late to back out? Calm down stupid, you're being ridiculous.

She jumped when the doorbell rang and her heels clattered on the hard-wood floor as she raced to greet her guest. "*Just breathe.*"

With raised eyebrows, her hired date whistled, "Saint—you've been holding out. I had no idea you could look like that." She felt her cheeks heat at the compliment.

"Well—I'm impressed about what a little hair product and a tux can do for you, Hollingsworth."

He flashed his million-dollar smile at her and closed the space between them to escort her to his navy blue King Ranch Super Duty F-350 and then opened her door to help her inside. The interior still smelled of new leather. "Dang, I'm a little envious of this ride." Some women would have preferred a sleek, low-slung car—but not Savanna, trucks were her thing.

He glanced sideways and shook his head. "It is still an enigma to me that *you* of all people would have to barter with someone to find a date to a wedding. It's….. pathetic!" He said it as though he was searching for the right description of her life.

She slugged his arm with her fist, "Cash Hollingsworth, I'm gonna slap you to sleep, and then slap you for sleepin." He chuckled at her as he drove down the driveway toward the dreaded destination—her cousin Rachel's wedding.

She couldn't believe it herself, but that's what life had brought her—a colossal piece of pathetic. Somehow, she had ended up at age forty, divorced and childless and to top it off, she had just watched a video about how divorced and single women in their forties are out of luck finding love. Their SMV or sexual market value is zero. Men in their forties however, are just hitting their stride. She rolled her eyes at the thought of it and zoned out the window as they rode to the venue.

~Rachel's Wedding~

Cash turned into the parking lot of the wedding venue and Savanna's stomach knotted. He pulled the large truck to the front entrance and the valet opened her door to help her out. His six feet- four inch frame dwarfed the valet as he came around to the other side of the truck.

The fall air was crisp and cool, typical November weather in Georgia. With her arm linked through his, they entered the venue of her cousin's wedding. It was a black-tie affair, complete with an orchestra and beautiful surroundings. The scent of fresh roses lingered throughout. An orchestra played the song, *A Thousand Years,* as an usher guided them to their seats.

Rachel, two years younger than Savanna, resembled a model in a bridal magazine in her wedding dress. She had found her soul-mate, a former military physician turned business mogul after losing her first husband overseas in a military training exercise. Rachel had one son from her previous marriage. Savanna was ecstatic for her and could recall pleasant memories growing up together. Although Savanna was the youngest of four siblings, Rachel had been the closest thing to a sister she had ever known.

Savanna whispered to Cash, "It's her second wedding, but Rachel's parents have obviously spared no expense. I'm sure the mother of the bride had been planning this day for a long time. Her family can easily afford it...they've made a fortune in the oil business." The music drowned out the rest of her whispered narration to Cash.

At the reception, Cash led Savanna to their assigned table and held her chair for her. She couldn't help but notice the father of the bride, her Uncle Phillip, who was her father's younger brother, scowling in her direction. Savanna smiled and waved. He gave her a curt nod. She noticed a chill in the air, but it wasn't because of the fall weather. Although she was the family outcast, Rachel still invited her to this wedding.

Savanna knew that if she showed up to this lavish event without a date, it would have been the ultimate humiliation. A part of her didn't want to miss the wedding because she wanted to partake in Rachel's joyous moments. Her cousin had always been a kind soul and deserved happiness. This event reminded her she still wanted to belong to a family… to belong somewhere… to someone.

Rachel and the groom, Dr. Bear Covington, took the dance floor for their first dance as husband and wife. When the dance ended, he dipped Rachel, and the guests cheered. Sparks were obvious between the two. The reception was perfect as expected.

Cash and Savanna exchanged small talk with their table-mates. Out of the corner of her eye, she spotted her Uncle Phillip and Aunt Marcia making their way toward her. Nervous with dread, she looked over at Cash and whispered, "Show time!"

Savanna and Cash stood and greeted them. Aunt Marcia hugged her. "Well now, don't you look stunning," Aunt Marcia drawled with faux warmth as she pulled back from the embrace.

"Thank you Aunt Marcia, it's good to see you," Savanna lied. "This is my date, Cash Hollingsworth."

Cash extended a hand to her Uncle Phillip and Aunt Marcia. "I'm pleased to meet you both. It's a lovely wedding." His voice was deep and charming as usual.

Her uncle pierced her with an icy glare, "I'm surprised you showed up to a family event. I guess you had nothing better to do. We'd better keep an eye on the silverware and wedding gifts while you're around. We wouldn't want them walking off."

Savanna's mouth dropped open and her face reddened. She didn't respond and hoped that Cash hadn't heard the exchange while he was entertaining her Aunt Marcia.

Aunt Marcia was enjoying Cash's attention as she tilted her head to the side and bragged with a coy smile, "I planned this entire event almost single-handedly."

Uncle Phillip rolled his eyes and excused himself from the conversation to mingle with other guests before Savanna could reply to his abrasive remarks.

"So tell me, how did you and Cash meet?"

Savanna choked on the Champagne she was sipping as she had not properly prepared for probing questions. She couldn't admit to her aunt that she had traded babysitting Cash's twelve-year-old daughter for a date to this wedding.

As if that were his cue for mercy, Cash interjected to tell the story…*a story*. "Well... Savanna and I met when she was in the military at one of the Air Force bases overseas." He gazed into Savanna's eyes for a second. "Even though we could not be together because of logistics, we've kept in touch over the years, and when I moved back to Georgia a few months ago, we reconnected and so…. here we are." He gave a fake chuckle and pulled Savanna close to him while looking into her eyes again.

To Savanna's relief, the explanation seemed to satisfy her aunt. "Well, that is just wonderful Savanna. We were wondering if anyone would even want you at your age," and laughed to make it sound more innocent. "The fish in the sea are more like icky puddles with tadpoles, at your age of forty. Although, you are aging well. Keep up the Botox or—whatever it is you're doing. You'll need all the help you can get." Her Aunt Marcia gave another fake and venomous laugh, "If you'll excuse me, I have some guests to entertain. It was lovely seeing you and Cash this evening."

Those words felt like barbed wire. Cash grabbed her hand as he witnessed the verbal attack on the woman he'd escorted. Savanna smiled up at him, trying to hide her embarrassment. She mouthed the words, "Thank you" to Cash as he led her to the dance floor. She couldn't help but notice several of the single and married women looking in Cash's direction with unabashed admiration. The video about sexual market value must be spot-on concerning men his age. Cash was for sure a man in his prime… aged to perfection.

A few of the St. James side of the family whispered while looking in her direction. "I can't believe she showed up here."

Savanna heard them and turned to Cash to see a puzzled look on his face. She shrugged and gave him a tight-lipped smile.

A child about age five held her sister Jenna's hand and Savanna saw the resemblance. It was Jenna's daughter. The girl bounced around and her brown ringlets bounced with her. Jenna turned to speak with another guest, and her daughter roamed the room until she made her way to Cash and Savanna's table. "Hi," she said to Cash. "I have a new dress and it twirls real big. Wanna to see it?"

Cash smiled over at Savanna. "Sure, let's see how your dress twirls."

The little girl twirled as if she were doing an arabesque in a ballet with her hands joined in an arc over her head. Her dress floated outward as she turned. "See, it twirls really big! Do you like it," she asked Savanna.

"I love it. You look beautiful in that dress," Savanna said.

The little girl said nothing but beamed up at them while holding her dress out at the sides. She was moving her little body back and forth when Jenna found her at their table.

"Don't wander off from me, do you hear," Jenna said to her child and then looked at Savanna. "Keep away from my daughter. I don't want you speaking to her ever again," and walked away with her daughter in tow.

Savanna glanced at Cash to see a bewildered look on his face. She didn't offer any explanation but gave another tight-lipped smile and looked away in humiliation.

"Care to dance?"

She took his hand and walked to the dance floor. Cash acted as if nothing odd had happened, but stayed by Savanna's side throughout the reception as if to guard her from further attacks.

When the reception was over, Savanna was so relieved to hoist herself into the truck and be on her way home.

Cash was quiet on the way out of the parking lot, and after a few miles down the road, glanced sideways at her. "So, do you mind telling me why your family is so hostile to you?"

Savanna gave half a smile and glanced over at him. "I don't know what you're talking about," she joked. He gave her a serious look, and she asked, "You sure you want to hear this?"

Staring out the windshield, he said, "Uh- after what I just witnessed—I'm dying to know what you did to deserve that kind of treatment."

She gazed out at the window and exhaled. "I was the youngest of four. First, there was Sam, my oldest brother and then Jaxon and then Jenna, five years older than me. Sam and Jenna were my parent's golden children and Jaxon and I were the disappointments. I'm not sure what we did to be unlovable but that's how it was growing up. Jenna was a petite brunette who aimed to please my parents and thrived on their praise. She was like an extension of them."

At my height of five-feet-nine, they made fun of me constantly. They would call me things like, "Baby Huey."

Cash looked at her and smirked, "You mean that cartoon character of an over-sized baby duck with a low IQ?"

She nodded and laughed. "That's the one."

"For most of my life, I've felt unattractive, stupid and unlovable, because of their insults during my childhood.

When I was eighteen, I was a natural brunette, and to rebel against my parent's control, I had a friend's mom bleach my hair to platinum blonde. It took an entire weekend to get the right shade." She smiled as she recalled it.

"I can't explain it, but when I saw myself with that new blonde hair, I felt a sense of freedom. That evening, I had forgotten about my new hair and my mother caught sight of me in the kitchen. I can still hear those words, *'Looks like we raised a bar-fly, well congratulations—to me! G.W. get in here and look at this girl who used to be our daughter.'*

My dad came into the kitchen and stared at me, '*You look like a slut. You always were worthless. Why couldn't you have turned out like Jenna?*' Then he stormed out of the house and peeled out of the driveway."

Cash looked at her with his hands on the wheel, "Saint… I don't know what to say…. that would have been harsh for a teenager to hear."

Savanna nodded, "It was—but I had become numb at that point. My mother pulled my hair so hard that evening, my scalp bled. I didn't fight back, but just waited for her tirade to end."

"That evening when she left for a dinner party, I swiped some cash from my dad's office drawer, one or two thousand dollars, I can't remember, and some jewelry as a parting gift." Savanna gave a wicked grin at the thought. " I packed my things and left without ever looking back. The only personal things I took were a few clothes and a letter I had written to *my future husband*." She laughed, and he smiled at her.

"A note to your future husband?" His tone was mocking as he always enjoyed giving her a hard time.

"Doesn't everyone write a letter to their future spouse," she asked with faux innocence, already knowing his answer.

"That's a big *NO* for me." He made a face as if the notion was ridiculous.

"Anyway, I moved out before I even finished my senior year of high school. That's when I decided to join the Air Force and become a registered nurse. I was in Germany when both my parents died in an accident." Her voice faltered, "When my siblings called me in Germany to tell me about my parents' deaths, I told them they were already dead to me. I didn't even try to attend their funeral. That's why my Uncle Phillip and Aunt Marcia and the rest of the St. James family members have such disdain for me.

I don't know what lies my parents told my family about me over the years, but I'm certain it would have been to cast themselves in a good light and make me look like a heathen. I'm sure they told everyone how I was a thief…. money grubber who abandoned the family." She gave a sarcastic grin at the thought of it all.

Cash stared at her when they reached a stoplight. "I'm so sorry, I never knew that about you."

She looked at him, "Well, it's not exactly something to start conversations with and it's not a great background. I've always felt shame." She laughed, "I bet you had no clue that your side of the bargain would be so….interesting."

With compassion he said, "Saint, you're a beautiful person inside and out. Don't let anyone ever tell you otherwise." He grinned, "Besides, my daughter adores you."

"I adore her too."

"It's not your fault you were born into an abusive family," Cash reassured her.

"I always dreamed about having a mother and father who loved me. I feel like I missed out on so much when I see other families so close and loving…even with their flaws. Sometimes I feel like I must have done something bad in my young life to have deserved it. I'm just hoping for brighter days ahead. I think God has a plan for me—when the time is right, I'll be the person I'm supposed to be…. then I'll meet the man and family I'm destined to be with."

Cash looked at her and said, *"Every one may not be good, but there's always something good in everyone, judge no one shortly because every saint has a past and every sinner has a future, by Oscar Wilde."* He topped it off with a teasing grin.

A smile spread across her face. "I like that, especially because you call me *Saint*."

After a second of silence, she said, "I guess Oscar Wilde wrote that just for me."

"You know it—*Saint*." Cash squeezed her hand and gave her his perfect toothed smile. "I quoted that to Kate the other day, and she said I was a dork."

"Imagine that," she said with sarcasm.

~Chapter 2~

~The Actual History of How They Met~

The story Cash told her Aunt Marcia at Rachel's wedding was true, as they really had met in Germany, but their relationship was *never* romantic.

The United States Air Force stationed Savanna at Ramstein Air Force Base in Germany, and she worked as a registered nurse in the intensive care unit at Landstuhl Regional Medical Center while caring for wounded soldiers.

Cash was one of her wounded patients. He took blunt force to the abdomen when a rocket-propelled grenade struck a nearby truck, hurling one of his troops and him into the side of a building. The blunt trauma to his abdomen caused severe internal hemorrhaging and the impact fractured his femur. A rescue unit transported him from the scene to her military hospital and saved his life.

He spent a few weeks in her hospital unit before being transferred to the states, and because of the blood loss, he required multiple blood transfusions, which required a lot of her time at his bedside.

When he was conscious, and in between the pain meds, they talked about how they were both from Georgia and eventually realized that they had grown up less than an hour's drive from one another. He told her he was in love and engaged to marry a girl named Amy.

Savanna and Cash were both officers in the military at the time and agreed to connect once they were stateside. He wanted Savanna to meet his soon-to-be wife.

Maybe it was because of the life and death situation, or maybe it was because they found out they had grown up near each other that they formed a solid bond and friendship during his hospitalization in Germany.

On the day that Cash was being loaded up for air transport back to the states, he took Savanna's hand and thanked her for the comfort she had brought to him. "I wish you could meet my older brother, Duke. He's in the Navy.

He's not as handsome as I am though." He flashed his perfect smile at her and added, "Hey—maybe we'll all meet up in Georgia sometime." He squeezed her hand.

"Take care, Captain St. James." She smiled back at him.

"Godspeed, Captain Hollingsworth." She felt his warm hand slip from hers as they moved the stretcher.

With a twinge of sadness, she watched the transport crew wheel his stretcher down the corridor and a part of her wished that they *would* meet up again. She brushed a tear from the corner of her eye and hoped that he would get to marry the girl who was waiting for him back home—just as he had planned.

~Chapter 3~

~The Reunion~

Years later, she was in Perkins Hardware Store in Glenn Oaks, Georgia and heard a familiar deep voice behind her.

"St. James?" Savanna turned around to see a handsome forty-something man standing there. He was looking down at her, beaming with a welcoming smile, while wearing worn, faded jeans, and a button-down shirt and boots. She felt a sudden burst of joy at seeing her friend from years ago. They *had* reconnected after all those years…. in a hardware store.

She inhaled a sharp breath while placing a hand across her chest. "As I live and breathe… if it isn't Cash Hollingsworth from Germany!"

He held his arms out and she hugged him. "You look amazing," she said. He loosened his hold and looked down at her.

"You look great too… the same slim, tall blonde that I remember from Germany." Cash said and she felt her cheeks flush.

"I can't believe it's really you! What in the world are you doing in Stillwell County?"

"My brother and I inherited some land near here, and I'm building a house on the acreage. I have some cattle and horses." He smiled, "I'm also retired from the military."

He was about to inquire about Savanna's life when a young girl with long chestnut hair came out of the restroom and tugged on his shirt. "Dad, I'm back." The young girl looked from Savanna and back to her dad.

"Savanna, I'd like you to meet my twelve-year-old daughter, Kate."

Savanna looked at her with surprise. "Hi Kate, it's a pleasure to meet you."

Kate gave a small wave. "Hi," she said with shyness.

They were moving out of the way of patrons to continue their conversation. Kate was growing restless standing there.

"Savanna, would you like to meet us down at Momma Lynn's Café for some iced tea and pie? We are obviously in the way here." His voice still held the southern charm she remembered.

"I would love to, I'll meet you both in a half-hour?"

"Sounds perfect. We'll meet you there."

~Momma Lynn's Café~

She checked her blonde ponytail in the rear-view mirror and smeared on some lip gloss before making her way into the café. Savanna's plain white T-shirt was tucked into worn Levi's with a pair of worn, brown boots. Cash and his daughter were sitting in a booth next to each other, and they left Savanna the seat across from them. She waved and made her way over to their booth.

The owner of Momma Lynn's Café made her way over to their table. She was a sweet, retirement-aged woman with a short gray bob whom everyone in town called Momma Lynn.

"What can I get for y'all," Momma Lynn drawled. Savanna and Kate had ordered tea and Peach Cobbler. Cash opted for the cherry pie. "Okay, that sounds real good, I'll have it out'n a jiffy." She smiled and walked away to retrieve their orders.

"So—Savanna St. James," he said in a deep smooth voice, "What have you been doing with your life since I last saw you in Germany?"

Savanna smiled and looked down at her clasped hands, which were resting on the table. She looked back up to meet his gaze. "Well, I stayed in the Air Force after I last saw you and then retired two years ago from the military. I saved some money during that time, so I came back home to Georgia, bought almost ten acres of land here in Stillwell County and built a modest, rustic style home right in the middle of it. It's my little slice of paradise and I'm happier than a tornado in a trailer park." Cash laughed at her.

"Any relationships to tell about?" Cash inquired.

Momma Lynn returned to their table with iced tea and freshly baked pie. Vanilla ice cream melted down the sides of the peach cobbler and cherry pie and they all three stopped conversing to dig in to the flaky deliciousness.

Kate had eaten half-way through her pie when her friend walked in the door. "Dad, I'll be right back, I need to go say hi to Abby." Cash gave a nod while shoveling the next bite of cherry pie and ice cream into his mouth.

"About those relationships?" He asked with his mouth half full. Savanna put her fork down and her lips pulled into a full smile at his persistence in wanting to know the details of her life.

She told him about her short-lived marriage to a pilot whom she had met during one of her deployments. "Six months after we married, I found out that he had been cheating on me. Accompanied by the cheating, was the beginning of verbal and physical abuse. He was moving up in the political circles and was best friends with some judges and the DA. I was too afraid to challenge him in any way. I knew I would lose in a court battle and even worse, could lose my life. Once, he even bought me an expensive diamond wreath necklace to apologize for one of the many episodes, but I soon realized I wouldn't survive if I stayed."

Savanna left out some painful events as she didn't think Cash needed to hear all the details of her dark past. "I eventually moved back to Georgia and changed my married name to my maiden name to escape the memory of that nightmare." She shivered at the thought of him. None of her family except for her cousin Rachel had known about that marriage or her divorce. She had put it all behind her and moved on with her life.

Cash could see the angst on her face reliving those memories. "Savanna—sounds like you've been through hell and back—I'm so sorry that happened to you." He ran his hands through his hair. "I can't believe some bastard could do that to you."

"Thanks for the sympathy. I can't believe I ever tolerated it or even picked someone like that."

"Whatever happened to him?"

"I know that initially he was with another woman, which meant that he would abuse her and not me. They later sent him to prison for transporting loads of cocaine in his aircraft. It's a relief to know he's behind bars. Hopefully, some *Bubba* in prison will take a shine to him." They shared a laugh at her remark and she was eager to shift the subject to something else.

"What about you? Did you marry Amy when you came back to the states?" Savanna took another bite of Peach Cobbler and waited for his answer.

His face became solemn. "Yeah—I did." He took a swallow of iced tea and looked at her. "I married Amy a year after I returned to the States. We were crazy in love and had a relationship that lasts lifetimes. My daughter was born seven years after we married. They stationed us in California when Kate was just a year old."

He paused and stared out the window. "A bullet hit and killed Amy as she loaded groceries into the back of the car." Savanna gasped and placed her hand on his. "Oh, Cash—I'm so sorry," she said.
"Who would have done that?" Her voice was soft.

"It was part of a gang who was attempting to kill someone else on behalf of a drug lord. Amy and Kate were in the wrong place at the right time." His eyes showed heartache and his voice held unmistakable grief and bitterness. He rolled the tea glass between his hands as he talked.

"I plan to avenge her death. Her killers will not go unpunished." He reddened and his jaw clenched after he spoke those words.

Savanna knew that he had been in Special Forces and the CIA, and suspected he knew how to find and kill if the situation arose. Her instincts gave her an uneasy feeling about his seething vengeance.

"What do you plan to do?" She took a sip of her tea.

Cash looked at her, "I'm not a man who backs down from a challenge. The California Bureau of Investigation kept telling me they hit dead ends, but my gut instinct tells me that there was some corruption and a cover-up. To my knowledge, they had never closed the case, and I had heard nothing from them in years. Then, a few weeks ago, Bryan, an Intel buddy of mine, called to say that he believes he found the group responsible for Amy's death.

I plan to use my skills and connections to find out what else I need to know. Then, I'll move forward from there."

"Will you leave Kate with family while you're in California?"

Cash shrugged. "I haven't worked out that detail yet. My parents have passed away and the only close relative I have is my brother, Duke. He's two years older than me and lives in South Carolina—retired Special Forces from the Navy." He took another bite of pie and swallowed. "Since Kate's in school, I have to keep her here." He raised his hands in a defeated gesture. His sleeves were rolled up and Savanna could see a tattoo of a skull and wings with the words DEATH BEFORE DISHONOR written to frame the image on his right muscular forearm.

"I need to figure out a solution...and soon." He said.

She tilted her head as if to study him.

"What?"

"No relationships for you since Amy died?"

He shook his head. "I can't even think about another woman until I've avenged Amy." She placed a hand on his. "Do you think that's healthy—I mean for you and Kate?"

"A mother taken from her family when her killers are free is not healthy. Yet here we are." His eyes flashed with anger and his tone was defensive.

"Cash—I wasn't trying to judge. I shouldn't have said that."

"Your intentions were good." The anger in his eyes changed to warmth.

~Chapter 4~

That evening, she sat out on her wrap-around back porch and watched the sunset. The conversation about her ex-husband kept creeping back into her mind. Tears were clouding her vision as she remembered what he had done.

Creed had thick, wavy, jet-black hair that he kept immaculate. It was a feature that stood out when she first met him. He had been so charming in the beginning. It was their first Christmas together as a married couple. The marriage was smooth and since Creed was away from home while flying, he wanted to give her a gift that would keep her company on the days he worked.

She remembered walking down the hallway in her plaid pajama Christmas pants, wondering where Creed had gone. She walked into the kitchen and he wasn't there. When she turned around, she heard little paw steps on the tile. She gasped when she saw what he had given her.

"A yellow lab! Are you serious, Creed… he's mine?" Creed nodded and smiled. She scooped her new baby pup into her arms. The soft blonde baby fur made her love him even more. He cuddled with her. "I'm naming you Brodie," she said as she cradled and hugged him.

In the weeks following Christmas, Brodie was succeeding at being house trained. He was growing and followed Savanna everywhere. He kept her company when Creed was away. Her husband became moody and she started taking the brunt of his outbursts. Brodie picked up on the energy surrounding Creed as he never petted her dog nor had anything to do with him. When the verbal abuse started, Brodie would growl at him when he would raise his voice at Savanna.

"You'd better do something with that damn dog or he won't live long, growling at me like that."

Savanna took his threats seriously. She tried to keep Brodie away from him as much as possible while hoping things would improve. He would bring her gifts and flowers as an apology for his unhinged outbursts and then repeat the same horrid behavior a few days later.

She had suspicions that he may be into some shady dealings with law enforcement and the judge. He would fly planes with unknown types of cargo on the weekends, and she knew to never ask about it. The last time she did, she ended up with a busted lip, and was told to mind her own business. She learned the hard way not to ask about the other women in his life or his dealings. Savanna longed to be out of the situation, even if it meant walking away with the clothes on her back and her dog.

His plate went flying across the room one evening, flinging grilled chicken and vegetables all throughout the kitchen. "This is not what I wanted. Is it too much to ask to get a filling meal? Are you too stupid and lazy to make something Italian? Look up the freaking recipe online, idiot!" He slapped her across the face with the back of his hand and looked at her as though she were repulsive. She would go numb and wait for the moment to pass just like when her mother would abuse her.

Brodie sat by her on the floor, letting Savanna hug him for comfort. His whine made her think he could feel her emotional pain. What would she do without this sweet dog in her life? What a blessing he was.

Creed's anger would come without warning. He'd be loving and nice one minute and the next, an enraged maniac. She dreaded when he'd be home. His job as a pilot gave her a break from his verbal and emotional abuse.

"When can we meet up again? I can't wait to see you babe…..yeah, I miss you too." He said to a woman on the other end of the phone.

Savanna stood behind him with her arms crossed as he talked on the phone to another woman. The fortitude to leave this unbearable man flooded through her and she was ready to stand up for herself no matter the cost. Tonight would be the last night she'd let him push her around.

"Want to tell me who you are missing?" He turned to see her standing there.

"It's none of your damn business. It's only a friend."

Savanna nodded. "Ok, well—I'll leave you to your *friend*. I won't be here when you get back. I want nothing. You can have the house and belongings. I'm getting a divorce." Her voice was quiet but steady.

Creed scared her but her determination gave her courage. He loomed over her. "You are nothing without me," he hissed. "You won't be able to make it on your own even if you have a career." He scoffed at her.

"I'm willing to try it. I'm a lot less *with* you."

"Don't be stupid, Savanna. I won't let you leave me. You belong to me." She turned to walk away but he grabbed her arm. She tried to pull out of his grasp and he twisted her arm behind her. "When I get back from Cleveland, you'll be here—or else."

She stomped on his foot to force him to let go of her and grabbed a knife from the kitchen counter. She felt a fire ignite inside her and she was ready to fight back. He let go of her and cursed her at the same time.

Brodie barked at him. "Shut up, you mutt! You'll pay for that Savanna." He gritted out the words as he rubbed his foot against his calf to soothe the pain from her assault.

His hand came across her face and stunned her for a second. He shoved her hard until her back hit the wall. Before she knew what was happening, Brodie came to her defense and attacked Creed as he tore a gaping hole in Creed's pants and tried to take a bite out of his man-parts. Creed shoved the dog until Brodie's paws were sliding across the slick kitchen floor.

Creed was enraged as he pulled out a handgun from the kitchen drawer. She saw him aim the gun at Brodie. "No, Creed, please don't! She lunged at Creed with the knife and punctured his right thigh to stop him from shooting Brodie.

Creed fired the gun. The dog yelped and fell lifeless to the kitchen floor and a river of blood pooled from his head. "No …. Brodie…. no. My baby!"

She forgot about Creed holding a gun as sorrow ripped through her. Her best friend had died trying to defend her. The pain in her heart was physical. Her body shook while laying her head on Brodie. The only unconditional love she'd ever felt was from this beautiful creature who now was lifeless on her kitchen floor. "My sweet baby boy is gone."

She didn't know how much time had passed. Her eyes scanned the kitchen. There was no trace of Creed. Her body was stiff and her heart ached with misery. Breathing was difficult as the shock and grief of the situation took hold. She remembered piercing her husband's leg with the knife and assumed he was fine. There was no trace of him or any blood other than Brodie's.

It was dusk when she buried Brodie under a tree in the backyard. Her arms ached from digging and she carried him wrapped in a blanket from the house to his grave. "Thank you Brodie for loving me. I promise you won't have died in vain. I'm getting far away from here. I'm so sorry for what you had to go through and I'll love you as long as I live." She wiped her nose and her eyes with a tissue and tucked it into her jeans pocket.

Savanna covered his grave and knew her next step was to move on to her next life chapter. Tomorrow she'd get the wheels in motion for a divorce and move forward the best she could. She knew that Creed had survived the knife wound to his leg and didn't know if he would try to press charges or get revenge on her. She wanted to file charges on Creed for Brodie's murder, but she thought her chances of escaping him would be better if she left without looking back.

    The sun had set and Savanna moved from the back-porch. She wiped her eyes after reliving those painful memories and vowed to stay strong and keep pressing on. Although her heart still missed Brodie, she was thankful that Cash and Kate came into her life.

~Chapter 5~

Savanna enjoyed the next few weeks getting to know Kate and Cash. She and Kate bonded over getting their nails done and shopping. They enjoyed each other's company. Amy's death continued to preoccupy Cash, and he had grown restless.

The afternoons were getting cooler in October, and Savanna loved this time of year. She walked down to the mailbox and opened the lid to find an elegant invitation with a gold wax seal.

Sitting at the kitchen table, she studied the envelope. Who on God's green earth would invite *her* to something? She took a sip of her lemonade, and wiped her hands on her pants to open the invitation:

THE HONOUR OF YOUR

PRESENCE IS REQUESTED

AT THE MARRIAGE OF

Rachel Caroline St. James

AND

Bear David Covington

ON SATURDAY, THE SECOND OF NOVEMBER

AT 6 O'CLOCK IN THE EVENING

57 EAST RIVER BEND ROAD

GLENN OAKS, GEORGIA

She felt elation for her cousin Rachel who had been so kind to her growing up. She hadn't seen her in years. "What mother would name her son, *Bear*?" She could just imagine the teasing he had endured as a kid…. Polar Bear… Grizzly Bear, Sugar Bear…. Care Bear. Her nerdy sense of humor caused her to giggle. *"Jeez—I need professional help."*

Savanna sat there and reminisced about the fun times she and Rachel had, which had been a reprieve from the abuse she had endured at home. She confided in Rachel about the harsh treatment from her parents but voicing her mistreatment made her worry about the repercussions of saying anything. Rachel swore not to tell because she was afraid to make things worse for Savanna.

She wanted to attend the wedding, but there was just one major problem. She was dateless. Other than Mr. Perkins, who owned the hardware store, she was smooth- out- of- luck. *Unless…* a smile spread across her lips as a new business proposal formed in her head.

~Chapter 6~

Cash leaned back in his chair with his arms crossed and his feet propped up on the table. They were sitting in his kitchen, which was still under construction. He grinned, "Ok, spill. What is this business proposal you have for me?" Savanna stood and paced the hard-wood floor. "Picture it… you get free food and champagne and you get to dance in a lovely venue—in a tux….with me." She raised her eyebrows and opened her mouth wide to fain surprise and excitement.

Cash raised his chin and looked upward toward the ceiling, "And what, pray-tell, do I get out of this barter arrangement?"

Savanna clasped her hands together under her chin. "Well, I'm so glad you asked. You… will have a babysitter for Kate so you can go to California for a few weeks, and she can remain in school."

Cash scoffed at her idea. "Let me get this straight. You will baby sit Kate for two weeks if I will be your date to a wedding?"

Savanna tilted her head and looked at him as her smile disappeared. "Yes, I am serious. We both very much need help from each other, and I think it's a brilliant idea."

Kate came into the kitchen since she'd been listening from the other room. "Dad, I would *love* to stay with Savanna for a few weeks while you go to California. Then hopefully, you can get mom's death out of your system, and for once, be present in the moment." The room grew quiet as Cash pondered that his twelve-year-old daughter had called him out on his unhealthy obsession. He relented and said, "Ok… it seems we have a beneficial arrangement." Cash shook Savanna's extended hand.

"You've got yourself a deal, St. James!"

~Chapter 7~

Savanna and Kate said their goodbyes to Cash at the airport just outside the security check-point.

"I love you Dad," Kate told him as she hugged him tight.

"I love you too, baby girl," Cash said and then looked at Savanna.

"Thank you for watching Kate for me. I'll be back in two weeks, hopefully with good news about all this. Take care St. James," he said, just as he had when he left her in Germany.

The jest wasn't lost on her, "Godspeed Hollingsworth," just as she had said to him when they rolled his stretcher away from her in Germany.

Cash was gone to California for almost two weeks when Savanna's phone rang. "Hello?"

"Hey Saint! How are my two favorite girls doing?" Savanna smiled at the sentiment. "We're doing great! Kate is finishing up homework and then we're gonna eat dinner."

"Oh yeah? What's for dinner tonight?" Savanna named off her fresh homemade rolls, corn on the cob, mashed potatoes and meatloaf.

"Dang, I'm missing out on all the food and the fun! Is Kate behaving?"

Savanna leaned on the counter-top. "She is the perfect kid. We're having a wonderful time. Would you like to speak to her?"

Cash paused. "Listen Saint—there's something I need to ask you."

"What is it?"

"I need to stay in California for a few more weeks. Would you be willing to keep Kate with you for a while longer? I'll make it up to you somehow."

Savanna straightened upright. "Yeah, absolutely, it's no problem, but are you in some kind of trouble?"

There was a brief silence. "I'm not in any trouble, but I have some leads and I'm making progress. I don't want to leave until I've taken care of business."

Savanna's intuition made her feel unsettled. "Cash, I—I have a bad feeling about this, but if you need me to keep Kate longer, I would be glad to."

His deep voice reassured her that everything would be fine, and she brushed aside her apprehension for his safety, and believed him.

Cash spoke with Kate and explained the situation. He told her he loved her, then ended the call.

Even though she missed him, Kate told him she was ok with the plan, to spare him any guilt.

Savanna was putting ice in the glasses, preparing for their meal when she looked up to see Kate with tears in her eyes and staring at the phone after she hung up.

"Oh Kate, honey, are you ok?" Kate nodded and wiped her nose on her over-sized sweatshirt sleeve. Savanna enclosed her in a hug.

Kate wept. "Savanna, you've been great, but I miss him. He's all the family I have here. It—like—scares me to think they might hurt him while he's away. He doesn't come right out and say it, but I'm afraid that... that he may be in danger and he's just not telling me," she said between sobs. "Just because I'm only twelve, does not mean I'm stupid."

Savanna loosened her hug and looked down at Kate. "You are definitely a very perceptive and smart girl."

Kate fidgeted with her hair and pulled her long brown mane to rest on one shoulder.

Savanna walked back into the kitchen and Kate followed. "Kate Hollingsworth, everything is going to work out just fine," she said as she tried to believe that herself. "Now, let's eat—I'm starving."

~Chapter 8~

~The News~

Her current work arrangement was ideal since she was caring for Kate. She was able to be home when Kate caught the bus for school and was home when she returned home in the afternoon. Savanna snagged a utilization management nursing job when she moved back to Georgia. She was able to work from home via computer, reviewing medical claims and medical records for a large insurance company. She was grateful for the calmness and decreased stress after all the years of dealing with trauma and the mental stress of emergency and intensive care nursing. Over the years, her career had taken its toll on her.

She dropped Kate off at multiple cheer leading practices, a school dance and watched her cheer at a few junior varsity football games. For the first time in her life, Savanna felt like a mother. Someone needed her and wanted to be with her.

One Saturday morning, they had their vanilla lattes in hand and headed to Sadie's Hair Shack. Kate decided she wanted a couple inches cut off her long brown hair and that it needed a few strategically placed blonde highlights.

Savanna's platinum blonde was a lot of maintenance, but it was her identity and her own personal symbol of freedom. She noticed that her brunette roots showed and she needed her hair done.

With foil on their heads, they sat and shared videos on their phones while waiting for the timer on the hair dye. The dog and baby videos had them cracking up.

Time had flown by as they enjoyed the day. The smell of cheese enchiladas and flaming chicken fajitas wafted through the restaurant at Desperado's that evening. "I'm going to need to walk a few extra miles this week to make up for this meal."

"You look great, Savanna, no need to worry." Kate said and laughed.

"I knew I liked you. We're gonna be great friends." Savanna said.

Pink and orange smeared the western sky, and the air was chilly when they returned home. The two of them were getting out of Savanna's car when they heard a voice outside the garage.

"Ma'am, are you Savanna St. James?" She heard a male voice at a distance behind her. Kate looked from the stranger to Savanna as she was about to walk from the garage into the kitchen. Savanna motioned for her to go ahead. "Kate, go on inside. I'll be just a minute." Kate shrugged and left.

Savanna reached in her bag to allow her fingers to skim the metal of her 9mm Glock as her instincts warned her to keep it handy. "Who wants to know?" Her reply was firm but polite.

"I'm Bryan Bentley, a friend of Cash's from California." As he spoke those words, her legs felt like they were going to drop her on the spot. Bryan stood there with sandy blonde hair and was physically fit. His right forearm bore a tattoo with his sleeves pushed up to his elbows. His tattoo was the same as Cash's. Careful not to frighten her, he narrowed the space between them and she remained planted where she stood. Savanna stared at him and waited in silence for the explanation of why he was on her property.

"I'm afraid I have some devastating news." He swallowed and his voice broke as he said the words.

Savanna stood by the car, frozen in place. "How did you know where I live?"

"Cash informed me of all I would need to know in the event that something happened to him while he was in California. I was there helping him find Amy's killers. I know that you took care of him while you were in Germany and that's where you met. We served in the same unit in the Army. He's been like a brother to me. I was close to his wife and was able to see Kate when she was two years old, not long after Amy died. Cash was a basket case after that, and parented the best he knew how. He told me you divorced an abusive bastard years ago, and that you retired from the Air Force." Bryan convinced Savanna he knew Cash, because only Cash would have known those details about her life.

Savanna looked down at the concrete on the garage floor then back to Bryan and asked, "What's the devastating news?"

He stepped even closer to her. "I'm sorry to tell you this, but—during a sting to take down Amy's killers, gunfire hit and killed Cash."

Savanna swayed and covered her mouth in disbelief. She thought the Mexican food that they had just eaten was going to come back up. "No." Her voice faded away as she shook her head.

"He died two days ago… I didn't want to tell you over the phone, so I flew down here as soon as I could. Cash left a will and instructions with an attorney in Stillwell County before he left for California." He placed an arm around her shoulder. "I'm sorry."

He turned her to face him and looked at her with his hands on her shoulders. "Cash's last words—*Tell Saint to take care of my girl*."

The weight of the news was heavy to bear. He stood there and held her. No one had *ever* called her Saint but Cash.

"Savanna?" Kate appeared in the garage doorway. "What's going on?"

Bryan stepped away and reached into his pocket. He handed Savanna a folded Manila envelope and told her that he'd be in touch if she needed him. "My information is in there." He pointed to the envelope. "I'll be staying in the area for a few days." He walked away. Savanna didn't see where he went, nor did she care.

Kate saw sorrow on Savanna's face. "Savanna… did something happen to my dad?"

She walked toward Kate, "Let's go inside."

She pushed the garage door button, then closed the kitchen door behind them. Feeling numb and weak in the knees, she walked into the house to tell Kate the unthinkable.

~Chapter 9~

~The Will~

It was Monday morning, the week of Thanksgiving break for Kate's school. Kate had eaten nothing for days since she had learned of her father's death. Occasionally, she drank water but mostly sat and stared out the window in her room. Savanna heard Kate crying herself to sleep at night and would lie down beside her to comfort her. Seeing Kate's grief made her heart ache. With all her being, she wished she could take away the deep, unbearable pain, but she knew that only time would lessen the sting of Kate's loss.

She and Kate had an appointment at the attorney's office, following the instructions in the envelope. Bryan also provided the information about Cash's will in the folder. She had no clue about his funeral wishes and was hoping to find out that information at the attorney's office. She remembered that Cash had one older brother named

Duke but didn't know if anyone had informed him of the tragedy. The nervous feeling in her chest told her she was about to find out.

They arrived at a brick building with a sign that said *Leland Owens Attorney at Law*. The sign was squeaking on its horizontal pole as it moved back and forth in the wind.

Savanna and Kate went inside where Linda, a woman in her mid-fifties, kindly greeted them. "Mr. Owens is expecting you. Please, come right this way," and led them down a hall decorated with fall and Thanksgiving decor.

His office smelled of pipe tobacco, which was pleasant. Leland Owens stood and straightened his tie as he saw them come in. Thick, but styled grey hair matched his mustache. Savanna thought he reminded her of James Brolin in his white shirt and black suspenders.

Leland offered his condolences once Linda introduced them. "Kate and Savanna, I'm so sorry for your loss. Cash Hollingsworth was a good guy. I first met him a few years ago when he and his brother Duke inherited their parent's land and oil wells here in Stillwell County. I had worked out some details for Cash and Duke."

Linda asked in a charming southern drawl, "Can I get y'all some coffee or sweet tea?"

Kate shook her and said, "No, thank you," and with politeness, Savanna also declined the offer. Leland waved her away in dismissal as she smiled and closed the door.

White knuckled, with her hands clasped in her lap, Savanna inquired, "Do you know if anyone has notified Duke of his brother's death?"

"Yes... yes, Duke has been notified and we are expecting him at any moment. He will be here for the reading of the will and for funeral arrangements." Her heart rate surged.

Linda opened the door and stood to the side to allow Leland's other client to enter the room. Kate was wiping her nose with a tissue when she glanced up to see her Uncle Duke in the doorway. She jumped up and ran toward him. "Uncle Duke!"

They stood there in a long embrace. Her arms were around his waist and he held her head to his chest with his large hand resting on the side of her face. His eyes were dull with grief. "It's so good to see you, Kate. You've grown!" He smiled down at her and then looked around the room to see Leland and Savanna standing by the large oak desk.

"Duke Hollingsworth, I'd like to introduce you to Savanna St. James. She has been Kate's caregiver for the past few weeks." Leland gestured toward Savanna.

Duke met her eyes and stepped toward her to shake her hand. "It's a pleasure to meet you, Ms. St. James."

Savanna was noticing how much Duke looked like Cash and he had the same deep voice. He was as tall as Cash and maybe even more handsome with more rugged features. Duke was the epitome of masculinity. Savanna was certain it wasn't toxic masculinity either. She could feel her face flush and admonished herself for her thoughts at a time like this. "Likewise, Mr. Hollingsworth… you can call me Savanna." She replied as she met his eyes.

Duke's eyes bored into hers. She couldn't quite decipher, but it seemed like he was challenging her. "You can call me Duke." He said with a half-smirk. Savanna nodded and smiled with politeness.

She fidgeted and straightened her periwinkle blue, fitted wool blazer. Leland interrupted her thoughts as he directed them to the oak desk. "I'll begin reading the will if you all are ready." He cleared his throat.

Leland picked up a stack of papers and read aloud Cash Hollingsworth's last will and testament. Three pairs of eyes fastened on him as he read.

The Last Will and Testament in the State of Georgia of Cash James Hollingsworth.

I, Cash James Hollingsworth, a resident in the City of Glenn Oaks, County of Stillwell, the State of Georgia, being of sound mind, not acting under duress or undue influence, and fully understanding the nature and extent of all my property and of this disposition thereof, do hereby make, publish and declare this document to be my Last Will and Testament, and hereby revoke any and all other wills and codicils heretofore made by me..........

Savanna could feel Duke's eyes on her and she glanced in his direction to find his icy stare. She refocused her gaze on the attorney in front of them who was continuing to read the next part of the will. *"What's his problem?"* She shifted in her chair.

As Leland finished reading the will, Savanna sat holding Kate's hand. Utter shock had claimed her senses.

Cash Hollingsworth had made Savanna Katherine St. James, Kate's legal guardian. Astonishment and joy filled her. She would be someone's mom. She belonged to someone, and someone belonged to her. In silence, Savanna stared out the window, lost in her own mental celebration and joy of what had just unfolded in the Law Office of Leland Owens.

Kate squeezed her hand, and Savanna came back to the reality of her surroundings. "I'm so happy," Kate whispered. "I have a mom for the first time in my life!" They embraced and shed tears of joy along with tears of mourning Cash's death.

Edward Duke Hollingsworth inherited all his younger brother's land in Stillwell County, including horses and cattle, along with the new house which was under construction. Duke was also bequeathed the navy blue King Ranch Ford F350 that Savanna admired. Money wise, he had fared well from his brother's estate.

Cash bequeathed Kate Vivienne Hollingsworth his life savings, of which she would gain at age 25. He had land rich in oil reserves in Texas, which paid dividends over the years. Unbeknownst to her, the inheritance would set her for life.

Leland looked at the three of them. "Do the three of you have questions for me?" Duke took a slow, deep breath and exhaled. He shook his head no. His face was expressionless and pale.

With a soft tone, Savanna replied, "No Leland, not at the moment, thank you."

Leland looked in Kate's direction "Kate?"

Kate shrugged her shoulders, "Um… no."

Leland cleared his throat again as if he were uncomfortable with the tension in the room.

Kate put her arm around her uncle's waist and his arm was around her shoulder as they left the building. Savanna's heels clacked on the concrete as she followed behind them. She felt an unexpected pang of self-consciousness, as if she were intruding on a private family moment.

The biting wind outside engulfed them and Kate pulled her jacket closer to chest.

"So—Savanna and Kate, I was thinking we could go get some food. Are either of you up for that?" Duke turned to face them both.

Kate nodded, "I haven't felt like eating for a few days, but I'm getting hungry."

Savanna suggested Momma Lynn's Café since it was as close to comfort food as they could get. "We can all ride in my car," she said as an attempt to be friendly toward Duke.

Momma Lynn spotted them walking into her café and ushered them to a booth. "Duke, Honey, it's so good to see you again," she drawled. "I'm so sorry about your brother." She patted him on the back as if she were his mom.

"Thank you for your kindness, Momma Lynn," Duke said.

"Savanna and Kate, how are y'all holding up," she asked as she took each of their hands. "We're doing the best we can under the circumstances," Savanna said for both of them.

"Well, whatever you all order today is on the house, it's the least I can do. Y'all better let me know if you need anything, ya hear?" She looked at the three of them.

"We'll keep that in mind, Momma Lynn. Thank you," Duke said.

They ate lunch as Savanna and Kate filled Duke in on all the activity of the last few weeks. Kate talked about her colt named Jesse, who had been born just before Cash left for California. She told him she had missed seeing Jesse as the situation had taken her away from the ranch for a while and how Cash and Savanna had reunited in the hardware store.

"Uncle Duke, will you let me out? I need to go to the restroom." Duke stood to let Kate slide out of the booth and sat back down as she walked away.

Anxiety washed over Savanna, and she wished Kate hadn't left them alone. Duke had the same look on his face as he did in Leland Owen's office—as if he had contempt for her. The lion was about to eat his prey.

"How did you become Kate's babysitter while Cash was in California?" He cut right to the chase, as if he wanted to waste no time while Kate was out of earshot. His dark blue eyes were piercing into hers as he waited for an answer.

Savanna almost panicked as she realized that no matter how she gave the explanation, it was going to sound lame. She glanced toward the hall that led to the restrooms and prayed that Kate would soon be on her way back to their table. He leaned towards her and she couldn't help but notice his scent and figured that it was probably expensive.

She found her backbone and decided to tell him the truth. *"What's he going to do, take away my birthday?"*

Savanna straightened her spine. "I.... told Cash that Kate could stay with me for two weeks while he went to California, if he did a favor for me. We each kept our end of the deal, but after two weeks, Cash asked if I could keep Kate a little longer, since he needed to stay in California for an extended period." Her hands gestured as she explained. "I told him I would be happy to keep her longer since Kate and I enjoy each other's company. She's like the daughter I never had," Savanna said wistfully, "and I think she also thinks of me as the mom *she* never had."

He stared at her. "What *favor* did my brother do for *you*?"

She held his gaze and said, "I don't think that's any of your business."

His face reddened, and a vein bulged on the side of his forehead as he exhaled.

Savanna congratulated herself on her satisfactory answer. She didn't have to give away Cash's part of the deal as her hired date to her cousin's wedding.

Duke stared at her with a smile like the cat who ate the canary. "So, you're the one who enabled Cash to go to California? Did you ever stop to think Kate that was the reason he stayed out of trouble? He wasn't able to be impulsive and reckless since she was in school and depending on him."

Savanna's mouth gaped open, and she felt her cheeks heat at his accusation.

"Excuse *me,* Mr.... *Hollingsworth...* but you are way out of line." Her voice rose. "You can't possibly think I'm to blame for your brother's death. I cared about him very much." Savanna realized she was raising her voice and looked around to see if anyone had noticed their heated exchange. "You have some nerve accusing someone you barely even know," she said in a forceful whisper.

Duke leaned forward over the table, locked eyes with her and pointed a finger in her direction. "That's my point exactly, you barely knew Cash or Kate… or me… yet here you are…. Kate's appointed legal guardian," he said with unchecked hostility. He kept his voice low so that no one could hear their conversation. "Don't think you're going to just sashay into our family and take over." His eyes held coldness as he added, "Kate is very special to me." The table shook when he put a hand down on the table. "Trust me, I'm not a man who will back down from a challenge." A glare accompanied his threat, but she held her emotions in check.

*"Where have I heard that line before," s*he thought, as she remembered his brother saying the same thing about avenging Amy's death.

"How convenient. Cash gave *Savanna-the-gold-digger*, money because of guardianship," he said.

She sat there with her mouth gaping—speechless.

As if the angels knew that she needed rescuing from Duke, Kate suddenly emerged from the restroom. She slid into the booth next to Savanna and placed her head on Savanna's shoulder. Her highlighted chestnut brown braid cascaded over her shoulder. "I'm kinda tired, can we go home?" Savanna reached over and touched Kate's head in a soothing gesture.

Duke motioned for Momma Lynn and she came over to their table. "Momma Lynn, the lunch was fantastic. We appreciate your generosity and kindness so much. I think we've got to get Kate home. She's tired."

Momma Lynn placed a hand on Kate's shoulder. "I meant what I said, if you all need anything, call me." She didn't let them leave without taking several pieces of apple pie. Savanna hugged Momma Lynn as they left the café.

She was grateful for the woman's authentic kindheartedness.

The three of them rode back to the law office in silence. Kate rested her head on the headrest in the backseat and closed her eyes in exhaustion. Savanna concentrated on the road in front of her as she drove them back. She tried hard to ignore the fact that her new nemesis sat beside her in the front seat. A storm of emotion was brewing within her.

A few silky blonde strands escaped from the chignon she had carefully placed that morning. The wispy soft strands were framing her face. She was so preoccupied with her thoughts she hadn't noticed Duke staring in her direction, as though he was studying every detail of her and making a mental assessment.

"What...no ring?" His inquisition brought Savanna back from her thoughts.

"What?" She was confused. He pointed to her left hand, which had been gripping the steering wheel.

"Not married?"

She glared at him and decided that the inquiry only deserved a one-word answer. "Divorced."

Duke seemed to bait her. "Mmm interesting." She found his smugness irritating.

"So, you and Cash weren't an item?" He was studying her reaction.

"No, we weren't…. ever."

"Hmm, also interesting." He looked out the passenger window, so she couldn't read his expression.

She hated that he looked so handsome with his perfect dark brown hair—longer layers on top and buzzed shorter on the sides. He smelled like fresh soap accompanied by a woody, light citrus scent. His suit and tie added to the medley of perfection. Even the scar along his left jawline gave him an edge. Once again, she chastised herself for thinking this man was attractive at a time like this. *"What is wrong with you, Savanna?"* She rolled her eyes.

His smile was arrogant, as though he had just read her thoughts, which only fueled her annoyance.

They pulled into the law office parking lot next to Duke's rental car. Kate opened her eyes as they came to a stop. "Uncle Duke, are you going to come hang out with us?"

Duke looked back at her from the front seat. "Sure, Kate," he told her in a calm voice. "I'm going to be spending a lot of time with you both." Duke glanced over at Savanna with a smile as he spoke, but she knew the statement contained a veiled threat, aimed directly at her. "I have to tend to some things that concern your dad's estate. Why don't you go home and rest and we'll catch up later this evening."

Kate nodded with weariness and smiled. "Ok—that sounds awesome."

"Ugh, I wish I didn't have to give this man my phone number and address." She moaned in her head but Savanna faked civility and gave him the information as it was necessary for Kate's sake.

He sent a text to her phone a minute later so she would have his cell phone number. His text said: THIS IS DUKE HOLLINGSWORTH—KATE BELONGS WITH ME. The words made her stomach churn. *"Why does everyone I ever care about always seem to... to leave my life?"* She reprimanded herself for her self-pity and drove Kate home.

~Chapter 10~

~Duke~

Duke was the embodiment of an eligible bachelor in his twenties and thirties. He had the characteristics on every female's wish list—tall, good hair and he was a man's man. Not to mention, when he was stateside, his mother tried to play matchmaker more times than he'd like to mention. He had no trouble getting women, and he had broken plenty of hearts.

But, Duke had one thing on his mind—being a SEAL. It consumed him. He lived, breathed, and ate BUDS training. Dating women was only a side gig when he was home. There was no way he wanted to settle down and enjoy civilian life with a little family and an SUV. He thought someday he'd like to raise a son or daughter, but for now, he was a warrior.

One evening, he attended a fund-raiser ball at the behest of his parents, and there she was—Calista Blakely.

She was tall with long blonde hair and a nice figure to match. Their eyes locked when she turned in his direction. He wasn't the only male in the room to crave her attention. There was something about her that made her siren-like.

Duke had always been competitive, and this girl presented a challenge. The two of them carried on a conversation with ease when he introduced himself. She was intelligent and beautiful—the woman that guys like him would settle down for. He could see kids and the picket fence with this one.

By the end of the night, she wasn't talking to any other men. The couple had been inseparable, and Calista loved telling people that he passed BUDS training and that he was a SEAL. Sometimes he wondered if she really understood the risk and danger of what he was about to do. She never acknowledged the possibility that he may not come back when he deployed.

They had fun together and intertwined their circle of friends and family. The day before he deployed, she told him bye and then left for a trip with her girlfriends. Duke was so focused on what was ahead of him, he hadn't noticed her absence.

He was twenty-eight when one of their missions ended with casualties and his injury. They treated him and sent him home for further skin grafting and treatment to his left shoulder and jawline.

His buddy fought along-side him as a sniper. He blamed himself for leaving his fellow soldier behind after he was wounded. They had each other's back in each gun battle. The military later notified Duke that his buddy had died in battle. *"If I had been beside him, he'd still be alive."* He blamed himself. He felt that he had abandoned his platoon, even though injury removed him from fighting.

Duke struggled with post-traumatic stress disorder when he returned to the states. He wanted to isolate himself, but his parents told him he needed to see Calista and he was hoping she could bring him some grounding and sanity. She arrived a day after his parents had visited. He was looking forward to her warmth and the closeness they once shared. The smell of her perfume wafted in as he looked up to see her face. He hoped the sight of her would bring him out of his dark place.

Her eyes closed in disgust when the nurse removed the bandages and heard an "ugh" escape from her lips. Her hand covered her mouth as though she was about to vomit. Duke excused her behavior in the beginning, as she had not been used to seeing blood and guts or wounds. But after a week, her coldness and distance became more apparent. She visited less often and made excuses. He didn't want to admit to himself that he was vulnerable. His career was over as a SEAL. The woman who he thought loved him, deserted him and found another man not long after.

"Things are different now," she had said. "I need someone who doesn't hide at home, but wants to be out and about in society. How are you even going to make money?"

Along with the burden of seeing some of his team die at the hand of the enemy, he was now facing rejection from a female because of his physical and mental wounds. He had no direction and no career plans. His mind was too overladen with the tragedies he had endured, and leaving the Navy also removed his identity.

After psychotherapy, and many skin grafting surgeries on his jawline, and left shoulder, he had improved. While the scars had not been as noticeable, they were still there. The trauma from losing some of his platoon in combat contributed to bitterness. After some time passed, a therapy dog organization for veterans gave him a chocolate Labrador support dog named Walker. His support dog helped, but it was easier to cope by shutting out the world and isolating himself. He became bitter toward women, especially tall ones with long blonde hair. He equated them all with being just like Calista.

His father passed away, and six months later, his mom passed. Numbness claimed his soul. Calista attended the funerals. No one knew that his parents had accumulated wealth over the years, but word got out and soon it had occurred to Calista that Duke was now a powerful and wealthy man. She started showing up where he would be, and she'd tell him that if he needed anything to call her. She showed up at his home and begged him to give her another chance. "I don't know what I was thinking," she had said. Calista became repulsive to him. It became difficult to even look at her. "Get your money-grubbing, power-grabbing ass out of my sight and please never speak to me again."

Duke was once tight with his brother, but Cash lived across the country in California when their parents died. After their mother and father passed, Cash moved to Georgia to raise Kate on the land he'd inherited.

Duke heard from him less and less after Amy's death. Justice and revenge for Amy preoccupied him. Duke bonded with his niece right away and always considered her like his own daughter. He hoped that Cash would find an excellent mother for her, but he doubted that was even possible. Women were only after money and what they could get out of relationships for themselves. Duke decided if he ever got involved with a woman, it would be transactional and not for love. He had no use for them other than the obvious.

~Chapter 11~

The first day in December, they laid Cash to rest. The day had been beautiful and sunny, but cold and emotionally draining. The memorial service was lovely and simple with military honors.

The locals of Glenn Oaks and surrounding Stillwell County attended, along with a few distant cousins and military friends. Duke wore his military dress uniform and had known almost all the mourners in attendance.

Savanna spoke to Bryan Bentley, the one who had delivered the news to her about Cash's death when he came over to offer his condolences. His eyes held grief and sadness. "Thank you for being a friend to Cash," she told him.

"Cash was one of a kind, and it was an honor to be his friend," he said to her.

She watched Bryan and Duke also had a brief conversation after the service.

They buried Cash Hollingsworth's ashes in Glenn Oaks cemetery near a Magnolia tree. He had no tombstone yet, but they had ordered one. Duke let Kate and Savanna decide on the design and the words on it.

Savanna and Kate laughed when they'd shared the quote he had told them both from Oscar Wilde. *"The only difference between saints and sinners is that every saint has a past while every sinner has a future."* They'd decided that it would be the quote on his tombstone. Savanna smiled as she recalled him telling her that quote.

In compliance with Cash's will, they were to have his late wife Amy's remains moved to Glenn Oaks Cemetery alongside her husband.

~Chapter 12~

Kate started back to school and was coping with the changes. She started eating again and could sleep through the night. Sometimes she would experience emotional break-downs, but Savanna, and even sometimes her Uncle Duke, helped to manage her grief.

Duke stayed in Stillwell County, near Glenn Oaks, to oversee the completion of construction on the house he had inherited from Cash. Kate spent time with her uncle there and enjoyed seeing her colt, Jesse. The horse was like grief-therapy for her. Duke cared for Jesse and ensured that Kate could see him whenever she wanted.

He avoided Savanna as much as possible. She knew he suspected her, but that wasn't anything she could control. She had Kate, and that's all that mattered. Savanna's heart sank with uneasiness about Duke's plans for his niece. Would he really file an injunction and try to have her legal guardianship revoked?

On Friday, as Kate was finishing her breakfast before school, she asked, "Savanna do you think we could get a Christmas tree?"

Savanna hadn't broached the subject yet, as she wasn't sure if Kate was up to it. "I think that would be wonderful! We'll go after school today if you like."

Kate's voice held enthusiasm, "Ok—I can't wait!" Her face was glowing with a smile and it thrilled Savanna. This was the first sign of any happiness for Kate since her dad died.

The clock on her computer showed 2 p.m. and Savanna had just finished saving her work when the doorbell rang. She was still wearing her heather grey sweatpants and an over-sized white sweatshirt. She had piled her platinum blonde mane atop her head with a clear elastic band that morning. "It's probably just the UPS man or a solicitor." She sighed, "I already know Jesus and I don't want to buy anything," she muttered the cliché to herself as she trudged to the door.

She peeked out the peephole and saw Duke standing there. "No! This cannot be good," she whined aloud. "What could he possibly want?" She patted her hair as if to improve her appearance. She looked down at her mismatched socked feet and immediately regretted not getting dressed for the day. "Oh, well—at least I brushed my teeth and put on a bra," she resolved and smiled to herself.

With her stomach doing somersaults, she peeled back the door to see Duke in jeans and a leather coat. He reminded her of a tall oak standing there. The north wind blew his hair, and the sky was grey with the threat of snow. "Hello Savanna," Duke greeted her in his deep male voice as she opened the door.

"Duke," she snapped. "What can I do for you?" She hoped her rudeness would make him want to turn around and go home. He looked past her into the house and back to her face.

"You can start by using some southern hospitality and inviting me in—out of the cold." She tilted her head and motioned for him to come in, and stepped aside to allow him entrance.

"Do come inside." She said with an exaggerated and dramatic southern drawl. He half-smiled and looked down at her socks as he walked past. His presence took up the whole entryway.

"Nice—socks." She looked down at her mismatched socks and then rolled her eyes.

He followed her to the kitchen which she had designed in white and grey marble counter-tops, a stainless steel fridge and white cabinets with black hardware. "Can I get you some hot tea or coffee?" Savanna asked with forced politeness as he looked around.

"Coffee. Black. Thanks." He said and took a seat at the kitchen counter.

She was hyper-aware of his gaze on her as she opened the cabinet to retrieve two mugs and tried her best to act like she was unaffected by his presence. She placed his mug under the Keurig coffee maker and waited for the coffee to brew. "So, to what do I owe the honor of your visit?" Her words dripped with sarcasm.

"You're honored by my presence," he said, to rattle her.

"Ye—yes. I mean no. You know what I mean," she stammered. She looked at him with frustration. "Why are you here, Duke? Kate's at school." Her patience was wearing thin. He looked at her with an arrogant and calculating smile.

"Wow... I really affect you." Duke appeared to be proud of himself as he leaned back and crossed his arms.

She exhaled with exasperation. "Hardly. You showed up unannounced during my workday when Kate's at school and you've yet to tell me why you're here." His coffee finished brewing, and she placed the steaming cup in front of him. Then, set her own cup to brewing.

"I'm here to finish the conversation we were having at Momma Lynn's Café."

Savanna looked to the side as she felt a stitch of dread. She crossed her arms in defiance. "Ok Duke—what more did you want to say? Did you think of more insults for me, because I can't wait to hear them," she fired at him.

"Well—first, you mentioned that you agreed to babysit Kate in exchange for something Cash did for you." Duke's eyes held hers.

She broke away from his gaze as she turned toward the coffeemaker to get her brewed coffee. She was thankful for the reprieve from his watchful eyes.

"What did Cash do for you, Savanna?" He took a sip of his coffee and waited for her answer with his eyes never leaving hers.

"Do you really think that is relevant to this situation? Why would you possibly need to know that detail?" She attempted a calm facade to hide her anxiety. She had already suffered a lifetime supply of humiliation, and she wasn't about to add to the burden by telling Duke that she had to hire a date to attend a family wedding.

"Why are you so defensive," he demanded. "I think I have a right to know about anything related to my late brother and my niece. Especially when it involves a person whom they've only known a short while, and ended up as *legal guardian* over my niece." He was losing patience with her. He controlled his tone, but his face reddened as he reminded himself of how Savanna looked similar to Calista, the woman who made him dislike women—A.K.A. power-grabbing, gold-diggers. He figured she had more than likely wrangled a significant amount of money from his younger brother.

Savanna was on the verge of giving him an answer, when the front door opened and a gust of arctic air filled the house. Kate walked into the kitchen and dumped her backpack on the kitchen table with a thud. "Uncle Duke!" She walked over and hugged him.

"Hey, Savanna!"

Savanna smiled at her. "How was your day?" She placed some homemade chocolate chip cookies on a paper plate and slid them across the counter. Duke and Kate grabbed a cookie and shoved a bite into their mouths.

"It was—like—long and boring, and I'm glad it's Friday," she said, while chewing with her mouth half-full. "Are we still going to get a Christmas tree this afternoon," Kate asked as she pulled the milk out of the refrigerator.

"Without a doubt," Savanna drawled with playfulness.

Kate looked to her uncle. "Can you come with us?"

Duke looked over at Savanna, "May I come with you?" Savanna had two people staring at her as if they were Golden-Retrievers waiting for a treat.

"Uh—yeah." At that moment, a pair of Hollingsworths had just railroaded her. Duke made her feel uncomfortable, and she was certain she'd rather have a root canal than to be in his company any longer, but she would do it for Kate's benefit.

Savanna took the time to brush out her long platinum blonde mane and give it some loose curls. She threw on her favorite crème-colored cashmere sweater and for added warmth, layered a white tank top underneath. She wore faded jeans tucked into some tall leather boots and had finished smearing on some deep berry lip-gloss.

"Hurry Savanna, we wanna go!" Kate yelled down the hall at her.

She shuffled down the hall while fastening her bracelet. Duke stared at her and his jaw tightened as she walked into the living room. She felt her face flush, and in her discomfort suggested, "Shall we go?"

They took the Ford truck Duke inherited from Cash. She realized as she climbed up into the front seat, that the last time she sat there, Cash had been driving her home from Rachel's wedding. Today though, it was the vehicle of choice for hauling a Christmas tree. Duke drove them out by the county line to the Wells Family Tree Farm.

Duke and Kate shared jokes and laughter while they searched for the tree. Savanna was quieter than the other two as she enjoyed listening to the banter between them. She was so thankful to hear Kate's laughter and even laughed out loud at a few of Duke's remarks. She didn't want to like anything about him, but her emotions betrayed her. Their mission to find a tree and the beautiful scenery lost her in the moment. She looked up several times to find him staring at her but assumed that he was summing her up…. as a gold-digger, or any other insult he could add.

They strolled through rows and rows of coniferous trees and the three of them finally decided on a 12 ft. Douglas fir. The farm-hand packaged the tree, and they loaded it into the back of Duke's truck.

Kate pressured her Uncle Duke into staying for dinner and tree decorating. Savanna had prepared a pot roast the night before. They were having roast, potatoes and carrots with cream cheese pumpkin bread for dessert. Savanna didn't have the heart to wish he wasn't staying because Kate loved having him around.

"I don't want to intrude," he had said, as if waiting for Savanna's invitation. She obliged. "Please… Duke, be our guest." Kate beamed at Savanna's invitation to her Uncle.

While Savanna prepared their meal, Kate and Duke sat in the living room playing an online game on their phones and yelling at each other in competition. Although Kate was just a kid and his niece, he still didn't let her win. "Yes!" He shouted when he had defeated her at the game. Kate feigned a sad face and yelled, "Cheater!"

When they finished, Savanna heard Duke ask where the restroom was and Kate warned him he would have to use her bathroom because the guest bathroom faucet didn't work yet. Thirty minutes later she went in search of them and found Duke's legs sticking out from the vanity in the guest bathroom. He found the tools she had left underneath the sink and began finding and fixing the problem. "Turn on the faucet, Kate." He yelled from under the sink. "Which one? Cold or hot," Kate yelled back.

A few minutes later, Savanna heard water running in the faucet and knew he had fixed the problem she had been trying to fix for a week. She had been ruminating about that darn sink and trying to find a solution. She walked into the hallway just as he was removing himself from under the sink and Kate was texting her friend in the hallway.

He sat on the bathroom floor and saw Savanna outside the doorway. "You fixed it," she said with excitement and appreciation. "Thank you so much." She extended a hand to help him up, and he took it, but made no move to stand.

"I'll help you up," she prompted. Their eyes met, and she leaned back to give him leverage to rise from the bathroom floor while pulling him with her hand. He helped their effort by pulling on the vanity with his other hand. They were standing toe to toe when he stood. She stopped breathing. Seconds seemed to go by before she broke the silence with, "dinner's ready," and left him standing there as she hastened to the kitchen.

After dinner, they went to the garage and pulled out all the decorations she had stored in Christmas bins from the year before. The three of them put ornaments on the tree for the next few hours while listening to Bing Crosby and Frank Sinatra. Time seemed to fly-by while they placed a garland on the mantel and put the finishing touches on the Christmas decor.

When they finished, the three of them plopped onto the couch with Kate in the middle. It was already dark outside with the time change and winter season. The beautiful white lights glowed in the darkness of the living room. They sat in silence to soak up the peaceful ambiance. Kate broke the silence. "Savanna, I'm going to go face-time Abby if that's ok. I want to show her our awesome tree."

"Yeah, go ahead. I'll make us some hot chocolate." Savanna said.

After Savanna served them hot chocolate, Kate said good night to them both. "Will I see you tomorrow, Uncle Duke?"

"How about I pick you up from school, and you can visit Jesse at the barn?"

Kate kissed him on the cheek. "Sounds good to me. Good night. Love you."

"I love you too, Squirt."

To Savanna's annoyance, she spilled hot chocolate on her crème cashmere sweater, and in a panic, hurried into the kitchen. She slipped the sweater over her head to treat the stain. She stood at the sink in her white tank top, gingerly removing the chocolate from the front of her sweater. She turned off the water and held it up to examine her work. Success! The stain vanished and she placed the sweater flat on the counter-top to air dry.

As she turned around, she didn't realize Duke was standing behind her and walked squarely into his chest, smashing her nose. She must not have heard him come in since the water had been running, and the stain had her preoccupied. He grabbed her upper arms to steady them both. She rubbed her nose and dropped her hand to her side.

He glanced down at her left shoulder and followed the scar down to her forearm, then lifted his left finger to trace the jagged scar. "What's this?" His finger traced the line. Her foggy brain couldn't register what was happening. She glanced at his finger as it traced her scar and somehow found her voice and regained her sanity.

She met his eyes and shook her head, "It's—that's a scar from when I was in the military." She waved her right hand in the air to dismiss the subject of the scar. Savanna cleared her throat and stepped away from his space.

She shrugged her shoulders and raised her hands as she spoke. "Um, thank you for going with us to pick up the tree and for helping to decorate, and I'm so glad to have the bathroom sink working again. I really appreciate you fixing it," she said in a cheerful voice to change the subject.

Duke's eyes still held seriousness. "You're most welcome. I guess that's my cue to leave." He studied her in silence. "You are definitely a mystery to me, Savanna St. James... a mystery that I intend to solve, since you're involved in my niece's life," his voice held an unnerving calmness.

Savanna looked up at him and folded her arms protectively. "There's not much to know about me, Duke. I think you're the one who's hiding something and you keep everything hidden from the outside world."

With arrogance, he said, "Hmm, I really didn't take you for a psychiatrist, but then again, you are probably full of surprises." He winked at her, "I'll catch your act later."

He headed out the door after thanking her for dinner and including him in their Christmas festivities.

She stared at the door after he'd left. *"Why do I have the feeling that he is about to disrupt the peace that I have carefully cultivated over the last few years?"*

~Chapter 13~

Shopping, and Kate's various Christmas parties, packed Savanna's week with activity. They attended the Annual City of Glenn Oaks tree-lighting ceremony and Kate played the flute in her middle school band's Christmas concert. Duke attended with Savanna. He wore a sports coat and jeans. Savanna couldn't help but notice his scent and how handsome he looked. If only he didn't hate her. She couldn't believe that he had smiled at her during the performance, because other than that, he had been indifferent and almost cold toward her. Her very existence seemed to irritate him.

They went for Momma Lynn's famous burgers afterward since Kate said she was starving. Momma Lynn had decked the restaurant with red cloth napkins on the table instead of the usual paper ones. The ambiance was festive with the feeling of home. Christmas music played in the background and the patrons were all engrossed in their own conversations and bursts of laughter.

Duke complimented his niece, "Hey kid, the music was great tonight!"

Kate looked at him with slight embarrassment and said, "Thank you Uncle Duke, I'm glad you liked it." She smiled and looked down to examine her snowman designed nails.

Duke looked at Savanna and Kate. "I was going to let you both know that I need to make a trip to South Carolina to check on things back at home." He paused, "And I wanted to see if Kate would like to accompany me when she's out of school for Christmas break, on the eighteenth."

Kate looked at Duke with elation. "Really? That would be—like—so awesome, I would love to go."

She looked over at Savanna who had remained quiet with a faux smile plastered on her face. Savanna felt like her heart was about to pound out of her chest. "Would that be ok with you, Savanna?"

A momentary silence followed. "Um… yeah… sure!" Savanna spluttered out her reply with a high-pitched voice.

Duke wore a smug, triumphant smile on his face as he looked at her. She felt the urge to punch him in his perfect face, but she refused to let him see that he had ruffled her. It was as if he were sending her the subtle message that he had won the first battle.

Savanna didn't want to keep Duke from his niece as Kate adored him, but her intuition was telling her that this trip to South Carolina was just the start of trouble that Duke Hollingsworth was about to unleash on her.

"When did you plan on bringing her back," Savanna said with ice in her voice since she wanted to throttle him.

Duke shrugged and replied with nonchalance, "Well, I was thinking we would return a few days after Christmas, around the twenty-seventh of December."

Her chest tightened. She could not believe that this Cretan was taking away the only family she had on Christmas! Yet, she didn't want to hinder Kate's happiness of spending time with her actual family during the holidays, so she kept her dashed hopes to herself. She'd suck -it -up and pretend to be happy for Kate. Savanna wasn't aware of what family Duke had in South Carolina, but she knew that Kate loved him and she would have to let her go at Christmas.

Kate was in the back seat, face-timing her best friend, Abby, on the way home from the café. She hadn't noticed the silent animosity coming from the front seat passengers. Duke drove in silence with a smugness. *"I would love to wipe that smile off his face,"* she thought to herself, *"but I would probably end up in jail, I'd lose my nursing license and orange isn't my color."* She sat there and sulked while gazing out the window at the Christmas lights. The lights were becoming a colorful blur as tears stung her eyes.

~Duke~

Duke glanced over at Savanna and his smug smile faded. He couldn't believe it, but he felt a stitch of guilt when he saw her looking out the window with her hands clenched in her lap. He almost reached his hand across the console and laid it on her hands as a token of comfort, but he thought better of it. He didn't want her to get the wrong idea. He had to remain objective about Savanna since she was going to be taking care of his niece, and he didn't know her yet. She was going to be Kate's legal guardian, but even more concerning was that she would be the person who would raise Kate as her own. Duke planned to remove her from Kate's life if she failed to meet his standards.

During his military career in the Special Forces, he had many successful but dangerous missions, rescuing and protecting others. This was one he could not afford to fail, for Kate's benefit.

The only problem was that Savanna was attractive with her long blonde hair and her long legs… and those eyes… blue-green… she seemed to have an attribute of shyness layered with an attitude with sass under the surface. He hated her type. *"She's the kind who's able to fool the average man. I am definitely going to keep myself in check for many reasons. Discipline. Yeah, thank God I learned discipline in the military. It pays to be a highly functioning sociopath… with a kind heart,"* he thought and smiled at his paradox.

~Chapter 14~

Savanna helped Kate pack for her trip to South Carolina. She also helped her wrap a present for her Uncle Duke and package it in the suitcase so it didn't get damaged during travel. She couldn't believe that Kate wouldn't be with her for over a week, especially during Christmas.

She felt shame and embarrassment that she had ended up in her forties, alone during the holidays. She would have been with Rachel and Bear, but they were with his family in Colorado this Christmas. How did that happen? She was also mourning the fact that she still didn't belong to any family. She still didn't fit into the Hollingsworth's and she sure didn't fit in her own family. Once again, she chided herself for the pity party she had just thrown in her head.

Kate's voice interrupted her thoughts "Savanna, are you sure you don't mind me going to South Carolina with Uncle Duke?" Her voice was soft and tears were welling up.

Savanna hugged her. "Kate… I want you to have a wonderful time. Besides, I'll be busy with work while you're gone and I'll probably just sit on the couch in my baggy sweats and watch sappy Christmas movies, while stuffing my face with junk food. I'll be fine! We'll celebrate together when you get back and take advantage of all the after-Christmas sales."

Kate studied Savanna's face and smiled. "Thank you, Savanna. I love you so much." Savanna felt the love and thought her heart would burst with it. "I love you too, Kate!"

Savanna watched as they left from the front porch and waved at Kate until they faded down the road, out of view. She swallowed the lump in her throat and walked back in the house to stand in front of the fire. An hour passed by as she cuddled up on the couch with her favorite over-sized crème colored throw and sobbed with unhappiness. To distract herself from misery, she made herself a cup of decaf hot tea and turned on a Christmas movie.

~Chapter 15~

She worked her usual company hours during the first three days after Kate left. It was Saturday, December twenty-first, when she cleaned the house as a distraction from her gloom. She cleaned all the grout in both bathrooms, mopped the floors, vacuumed and organized her closet, and scoured the kitchen with bleach. The cleaning products battered her hands. "A manicure is just what I need."

The cow bell clanked above the door of Lee's Nail Salon, downtown Glenn Oaks. A few of the customers were chatting with their nail technicians. Rose, her usual tech, motioned her over to a chair. "Hey Savanna! How is your Christmas going?

Savanna smiled. "It's great, thank you."

Rose pointed to the nail colors, "Which color you like?" Savanna handed her a nude colored polish with the name Pale Cotton Candy. She wasn't in the mood for anything with much color. She was feeling just…..blah.

    The Christmas music playing in the background was getting on her last nerve. Savanna wanted to sit there in silence. Nor was she inclined to disclose that Kate wouldn't be with her on Christmas. So, she engaged Rose in conversation with the goal of having Rose talk about her own life. It worked like a charm. The kind woman doing her nails talked about her own kids and what they wanted for Christmas, and all the places she had gone to shop to fill their wish lists. Another customer sitting beside them chimed in to talk about some online coupons. Savanna was in the clear about talking about her personal life.

    She was making her way over to the sink to wash her hands when she overheard a conversation. She recognized two women in the salon, Sydney and Ella. They had kids in high school and middle school and knew everything about everyone. The two of them seemed to be on every committee ever invented. They had been talking about people they knew who were getting divorced and people getting married. The name Duke Hollingsworth caught her attention. The two women were talking about what a shame it was that his brother passed and that Duke had been living in South Carolina. They prattled on that he was so "hot" and quite a catch, but he was engaged to someone in South Carolina.

Savanna wasn't exactly sure what to do with that kind of information….engaged? Was that why Duke wanted Kate to go to South Carolina with him….to meet his fiancé? What if Kate decides that the fiancé would be a better mom than she would be and then live with Duke and the fiancé? "Such—an—idiot!" Savanna hit her forehead with her palm.

Rose walked over to the sink with a concerned smile. "Uh, Savanna, is everything ok, you alright?"

Savanna jerked when she heard Rose's voice. "Oh… yeah!" She fake laughed. "I just remembered something I needed to pick up at the grocery store."

The two gossips, Sydney and Ella were eyeing her. After Rose finished with the manicure, Savanna paid and hurried out the door to the safety of her car and rested her head on the steering wheel.

Her depressed mood motivated her to be lazy and lie around on the couch all day watching movies. Cozy in her flannel drawstring pajama pants and a matching stretchy long sleeved T-shirt, she tried her best not to think about the grim situation that she'd just imagined while she was in the nail salon.

The clock on her cell phone showed nine p.m. Her eyelids were half-way down and cuddling up in her bed for an early bedtime, sounded like heaven. She closed her bedroom door and nestled in her white goose down comforter after switching off the lamp. The cool sheets felt soothing, and she drifted off to sleep.

"CLUNK." She wasn't sure if she had really heard it and laid back on her pillows and drifted to sleep again. The sound occurred again, but now she was wide awake and hoping it was just the wind. Her imagination told her it was something more sinister.

She looked at the clock which showed ten minutes past midnight. Her heart was now racing. Fear had seized her, and she couldn't will her limbs to move—and then adrenaline coursed through her. She opened the bedside table without turning on the lamp. The luminosity from multiple night lights enabled her to see. Savanna pulled out her 9mm Glock and tiptoed toward the door. She held one hand on the gun and one hand out to grip the door handle. Her moves were panther-like, advancing toward the door without making a sound.

Stabbing pain seared through her toe and foot as she tripped on a ten-pound hand-weight she had used earlier in the day. The hand weight rolled and hit the end of her bed with a loud thud and without stifling herself, she yelped out in pain. She hobbled and grabbed the end of the bed to steady herself with her free hand, while the other held the gun.

A moment of fear and intense pain had taken over, but she knew had to pull herself together. Her foot was still throbbing. She could ignore the pain as the adrenaline was still free flowing. Savanna mustered enough courage to advance closer to grab the door handle. Just then, the door flung open toward her, short of bashing her in the face.

Her heart felt as though it would escape her chest as terror gripped her. Savanna tried to control her shaking. She was certain she didn't plan on dying in her own home tonight without a fight. She took the gun in both hands and took a stance that would easily enable her to shoot first and ask questions later.

A large male silhouette was now looming in her bedroom doorway a few feet from her. The only lights behind him were from the glow of the Christmas tree down the hall. She couldn't hear any sounds since her pulse was pounding in her ears.

Before she could register what was happening, she felt a blow to her right arm as the gun flew out of her grasp. Her intruder had knocked the gun loose from her hands. She panicked when she couldn't budge the stranger. As they crashed to the floor, the intruder landed on top of her, pinning her right hand above her head and her left arm between them. The back of her head thumped the floor. A familiar masculine scent invaded her senses just as her world faded to black.

"Savanna." She could hear her name being called by a deep male voice, but her brain couldn't register her surroundings. She was being shaken. As she opened her eyes and the room came into focus, she saw Kate's worried face and Duke kneeling above her. "Savanna, are you alright?" Kate's worried tone brought her back to her surroundings.

Duke raised her head and shoulders to an upright position as Kate grabbed pillows from the bed and placed them behind her. She was still lying on the cold, hardwood floor.

"What… hap—?" Savanna's voice trailed off, and she tried again to speak. "What are you both doing here…in my bedroom… in the middle of the night?"

Kate and Duke looked at each other then back at Savanna, and in unison said, "We wanted to surprise you." Kate nodded to reinforce their statement.

Savanna raised her brow and replied with dry humor, "Well, I am definitely surprised!" The beginning of pain in her head got her attention along with the throb in her left foot.

She raised herself to a sitting position and leaned back on her hands. Her right wrist was sore as she used her hands to support herself. She gazed across the room to see her gun lying on the floor against the wall and shuddered at the realization that she had almost shot Duke. He followed her gaze to the gun lying there. "I almost killed you."

"Yes—I know." His voice held sarcasm.

"My hand to hand combat skills came in handy tonight. Years in the military and countless dangerous missions—but I don't think I've ever come as close to death as I did in Stillwell County, Georgia tonight." His face was stone cold to let her know he found no cuteness or humor in the situation.

"Sorry about that, but I wasn't expecting company at midnight. You woke me out of a dead sleep. How did you two get in the house?" She looked at Kate.

"I have a key to the front door, and I know the security code, so the alarm didn't sound."

"Oh… right." Savanna attempted to stand.

Duke pulled her from the floor with ease and she put her arm around his waist as he helped her hobble into the living room. She eased herself onto the couch.

He went around behind her and pulled the scrunchy hair tie that was holding her loose bun on top of her head. Her blonde hair cascaded around her shoulders. He ran his fingers through the back of her hair to feel for any blood, and he examined her scalp for any broken skin. "Other than the bump on the back of your head, everything appears to be intact." He cleared his throat and stepped away from her as though she were Medusa and he had just put his hands in a pile of snakes.

Kate brought her an ice pack and a glass of water. "Thank you, Kate." The cool water felt soothing on her throat. As Savanna held the ice pack to the back of her head, she heard Duke shuffling around in the kitchen and a few minutes later, he had returned with two tablets.

"Tylenol… for the pain." He handed her the pills, and she gulped them down with some water and leaned back. Duke put her feet up on the ottoman and examined her left toe. It was swelling and turning shades of purple and black. He placed a Ziploc bag of ice, which he had wrapped in a kitchen towel, on her foot.

Savanna looked at Kate and avoided eye contact with Duke. "I'm so glad you're here, but why did you come back early?"

Kate sat beside her and laid her head on Savanna's shoulder.

"I missed you and couldn't stand the thought of being away from you during Christmas. It would be our first one together. Since I was missing you so much, Uncle Duke said he'd bring me back and he would stay here in Glenn Oaks until after the New Year. I had a great time at his ranch in South Carolina, but I wanted to be here with you."

Savanna leaned over and rested her head on Kate's and said, "My cup runneth over."

We planned to be quiet since it was after midnight, but I guess we must have woken you when we set down the luggage," Kate explained. "After we got in the house, I had to use the restroom since I drank too much water on the way home. When I came out of the bathroom, I heard a commotion in your bedroom and—like—ran down the hall. Then I looked in your bedroom and saw Uncle Duke lying on top of you and you were out cold."

Savanna felt her cheeks heat at the thought.

Duke's face held annoyance and he said, "I heard a thud in your room along with a yelp and thought something was wrong. On instinct, I headed in that direction and opened your door… only to find myself at the wrong end of a 9mm. That's when I knocked the gun out of your hand

and tackled you before you could fire the gun." He looked at her with a smirk and added. "Lucky it was me walking through that door and not Kate. Lord knows what might have happened." His tone was acid and Savanna didn't like it.

Her smile was fake as she retorted, "For Kate's sake, I guess I'm glad I didn't kill you. She'd be without an uncle." He glared at her and she could see she had struck a nerve. A small bit of satisfaction made the situation more palatable.

The ordeal didn't irritate Savanna, she was just thankful to have them home. *"Correction—I'm thankful that Kate's home,"* she amended her thoughts.

The next day was Christmas Eve and Duke stayed at their house most of the day and came back the following day on Christmas. Kate gave him the gift that Savanna helped her wrap before she left for South Carolina. As Duke unwrapped the gift, he struggled to hold his emotions in check. The gift box held a duck call that she would have given to her dad. Duke knew that Cash loved duck hunting, and Kate wanted her uncle to have something that would have meant a lot to her dad. "Thank you Kate, this gift is perfect." He hugged her and she smiled with a sense of pride.

Kate surprised Savanna with a gift. "You didn't have to get me anything, Kate," she gushed and then opened the gift box to find a tan backpack with turquoise initials—S.K.S. "Thank you, Kate! I can use it for so many things." She hugged Kate in gratitude.

"I ordered it from Abby's mom at a discounted price, and I'm glad you like it." Kate looked pleased with herself.

After they opened gifts, the three of them pitched in and made Christmas dinner, complete with a juicy ham, dinner rolls, gravy, mashed potatoes, green beans and buttery yams. The house smelled like a home should smell at Christmas time. Savanna had even snagged a couple of apple and pecan pies from Momma Lynn the day before.

She stopped for a moment to take it all in and to count her blessings. The day was cloudy and cold with no lovely snow, but she had a home, a delicious meal and people to share this day with. She smiled.

Although her head and right wrist were back to normal, her left toe and foot was slower on the mend with bouts of swelling and pain. The bruising was still there and beginning to turn different shades. She hobbled around in the kitchen, chopping and cutting veggies until her foot throbbed.

Duke helped her to the couch and propped it up for her with a stack of pillows and an ice pack. He had even gone out to find some ibuprofen and scouted around until he found some at a convenience store. She hated that his kindness was affecting her and he was growing on her. She also thought his three-day beard scruff suited him well.

He was careful to keep his distance as much as possible while helping her in the kitchen or assisting her to get around in the house. She looked up occasionally and caught him staring at her. She'd just smile with politeness and return to her task. She was wary of him and his intentions.

Savanna's mind was on repeat about the conversation she overheard in the nail salon about Duke being engaged. No wonder he kept his distance from her. Why on earth would he leave his fiancé in South Carolina during Christmas though? She and Duke never shared personal conversations other than interacting when Kate was around, and it was for the best in her opinion.

~Chapter 16~

New Year's Eve was a week away and her agenda did not include ushering in the New Year at a party. Kate's friend, Abby, invited her to spend the night at her house on New Year's Eve as they were going to a party hosted for the tweens and teens at her church.

She wore a hopeful expression on her oval face as she begged Savanna to let her go. Kate was so excited, she almost knocked Savanna over with celebration when Savanna granted her permission to go.

This meant they had to go to the mall to find the perfect outfit. Five packed stores and six hours later, Kate settled on the perfect outfit. The bitter cold pressed on them as they made their way back to the car.

As Savanna was about to fling her fatigued body into the driver's seat, she heard a familiar female voice calling her name. "Savanna!" She looked up to see Rachel

Covington, her newly married cousin, waving her arms while trekking her way over to her car.

Kate stood shivering on the passenger side.

"How—are—you?" Rachel held her arms out for a hug as she reached the car. Her auburn hair bounced as she walked in high-heeled boots. "It's so good to see you again," she drawled.

Savanna greeted her with a warm smile and a hug. "How's married life?" Green eyes met hers, "I love it. We were meant to be. It's nice going through life with someone and taking on the world together."

Rachel clutched her coat to her chest. "So are you and Cash still an item?"

Savanna glanced in Kate's direction. "Uh...no, he passed away a few weeks after your wedding."

Rachel's mouth gaped open with sympathy. "I—I don't know what to say… I'm so sorry."

Savanna motioned for Kate to come around to her side. "Rachel, I'd like you to meet Kate… Cash's daughter."

She shook Kate's hand, "Hi, it's so nice to meet you, Kate. I'm Savanna's favorite, first cousin, Rachel."

Kate grinned and said, "It's nice to meet you, Rachel."

Snowflakes were dusting the cars in the parking lot. "You're such a beautiful girl… I'm so sorry for your loss."

Kate thanked her and then excused herself to scurry around to get in the passenger side for warmth. Savanna hadn't had the chance to explain to Rachel that she and Cash were never a real couple.

As the snowfall was gaining momentum, Rachel inquired about Savanna's plans for New Year's Eve. Savanna pulled her mint green cashmere beanie cap further down on her forehead and shivered as she admitted that she planned to curl up with a book on the couch and fall asleep, since Kate made plans to go with her friend overnight.

Rachel gasped as if that was inconceivable. "I realize you may still be in mourning over the loss of Cash, but If you need a date, Bear has a few divorced guy friends who would line up for the job… and it would be a shame if you stayed home!"

Savanna sighed and shook her head, "I appreciate the offer Rache, but I'm just not in the mood for ringing in the New Year."

As if that was not an acceptable answer, her cousin resorted to whining and begging. "Pleease come Saav… it's not normal to stay holed up at home… alone… on New Year's Eve… and you won't regret going. It's gonna be a gorgeous event, hosted by Bear's family. I'll email you the details… mmkk?"

Savanna relented with exasperation. "Fine." She gave a tight-lipped smile and hugged her relentless cousin goodbye.

She laughed to herself as she watched Rachel's petite form taking tiny, bobbing steps in high heels while rushing through the snow covered parking lot to escape the cold.

On the drive home, Kate asked, "So, Rachel's your favorite cousin?"

Savanna kept her eyes on the snowy road. "Yep, for sure. She's the only family member I was ever close to growing up, except for my grandmother on my father's side. Rachel and I called her Mee Mee Jane."

She snickered at she thought of a memory. "Our Mee Mee Jane was the sweetest person. She was also petite, but morbidly obese. There was this one time Rachel and I got to spend the night at her house. We found a pair of her panties. They were these white, high-waist, enormous…

things! I swear, they were about three feet wide and three feet tall." She used one hand to animate how big they were while holding the steering wheel with the other hand.

Kate laughed.

"We decided it would interest us to see just how far we could stretch Mee Mee Jane's panties across the room. So, Rachel found two yardsticks to measure the distance." Savanna held back laughter as she tried to tell the rest of the story. "Mee Mee Jane caught us and was furious. She grabbed a yardstick and started spanking our behinds with it. All while saying, *'What in tarnation are y'all doing to my pain-iz, I paid good money for those!'* We were running from her and laughing at the same time.

We also loved how she pronounced panties….pain-iz." Savanna paused. "Rachel and I eventually apologized to our Mee Mee, and she forgave us. We've always wondered just how much she had to pay for those big panties since she said she paid *good money* for them."

"Just for the record Kate, I was only a kid when I pulled that stunt. I would never make fun of someone's underwear now. I've grown as a person." Savanna laughed again.

"Right Savanna! I'd better hide my undies when I get home." Kate said with sarcasm and a smile.

Laughter filled the car for the rest of the drive.

~Chapter 17~

~The Invitation~

A red cardinal sat on a tree limb outside her office window, and snow blanketed the ground as she sipped her morning coffee.

She turned her attention to the new email she had received at six a.m. It was Saturday, and Rachel had emailed the information about the party, just as she had promised.

She had designed the graphics in gold sparkly letters, on a black background and included a note at the bottom:

Venue: The Waterford Hotel

Attire: Cocktail

Time/Date: 8:00 PM on December 31st

Hosted By: Covington Family

"Logan Garner has agreed to be your date. He's a 36-year-old divorcee who will pick you up. I hope you don't

mind, I gave him your address and cell number. He'll call you this weekend to confirm. I can't wait to see you there and thank you for agreeing to go!—XOXO Rachel."

Savanna laid her head on her desk and moaned. "What have I gotten myself into?" Slight humiliation terrorized her mind since she had to barter a date to Rachel's wedding. Then, her cousin had to arrange a blind date for her on New Year's Eve. Gratitude crowded out the embarrassment as she thought about how Rachel had gone to all the trouble to ensure she didn't celebrate alone.

New Year's Eve arrived, and Kate bubbled with excitement. She was waiting for Abby to pick her up. At noon, she jumped up and ran to the front door as Abby rang the doorbell seven times. She shoved her overnight bag over her shoulder, "Bye, Savanna! Love you," and bounded out the door without waiting for a response.

Savanna hadn't heard from Duke since Christmas Day, and she wondered if he had plans for the evening. Thoughts of his alleged fiancé loomed in her mind. Would this fiancé come to Georgia to ring in the New Year with him this evening?

"Why would you even care, Savanna," she admonished herself.

Logan called her and they had agreed that he would pick her up at seven-thirty. She had just finished putting the finishing touches on her make-up. Her blonde hair was in an up-do, swept to one side to accentuate her light gold, backless dress, which grazed her curves. She shoved her feet into her heels and grabbed her clutch just as the doorbell rang.

Her date was standing there with a bouquet of pink Ranunculus when she opened the door.

"Hi Logan!"

He smiled at her. His grey eyes met hers as he lifted the flowers in her direction. "Savanna, these are for you."

She lifted them to her nose to take in the scent. "These pink beauties are my favorite. Please come in." They exchanged small talk as she placed the flowers in a glass vase.

"Shall we go," she said.

Savanna took the arm he extended to her.

"You look gorgeous in that dress," he said as they walked toward his car. "We're going to make a good-looking pair tonight."

"I couldn't agree more and thank you." She smiled at him.

~New Year's Eve Party~

The Waterford Hotel ballroom had white fairy lights from floor to ceiling accompanied by sheer white draped panels.

"It's magical," she breathed as they walked in.

A live band playing Glenn Miller's *In the Mood*, gave a sense of celebration and joy as the guests arrived. The party goers wore cocktail attire and nibbled on Hors d'oeuvres while holding champagne flutes. Laughter filled the place along with animated conversations. After taking in the ambiance, Savanna was grateful Rachel had wrangled her into attending.

Logan and Savanna were trading stories when Rachel came over to greet them. "Logan, you're looking handsome as usual." She leaned toward him and tiptoed to plant a kiss on his cheek. He gave a crooked but charming smile. Rachel elbowed Savanna "I'm glad to see the two of you hitting it off."

"Thanks for fixing us up, Rache."

Arms wrapped around Rachel from behind as she was talking to Savanna and Logan. Bear joined their circle to say hello. She looked up at her husband sideways. "Bear, you remember my cousin Savanna from our wedding?" He nodded.

"It's good to see you here tonight." Bear gave her a wink, as if he knew Rachel had strong-armed her into it. Then, he looked at his buddy Logan, "Hey man, glad you could make it." They slapped backs as guys do and continued their guy conversation.

Rachel linked arms with Savanna as they surveyed the room. A tall male figure with dark brown hair caught her eye across the room. She did a double take just to be sure. Could it be? *Why would he be here?* Rachel looked at

Savanna and then traced her gaze to the man across the room.

"He's hot, don't ya think," Rachel teased.

"He's—D- Do you know who that is?" Savanna looked over at Rachel.

"Yeah I do, that's Duke Hollingsworth, an acquaintance of Bear's from his military days as a physician."

Savanna's question confused Rachel, "Why? Do you know him?"

"I sure do." She turned to face Rachel. "That's Cash's older brother."

Rachel inhaled and placed her fingers over her lips.

"He's not too happy with me since his brother awarded me legal guardianship over his niece. Duke thinks I enabled his brother's death. He also thinks I'm after Cash's money and—he hates me."

Rachel stared at her in disbelief, "You mean, Cash awarded you guardianship instead of his own brother?"

"Yep."

She spent the next few minutes updating Rachel on all the changes in her life since she met Cash and Kate in the hardware store.

Rachel took Savanna's hands in hers as they faced each other. "You poor thing," she drawled with genuine warmth and concern. "I can't believe he's being such a jerk to you!"

Logan and Bear joined them. "Everything ok?"

"I think we need a drink." Rachel took her husband's hand and ushered him toward a server who was holding a tray of full champagne glasses. Savanna knew that her cousin was about to fill him in on all the details of her life.

"Would you like to dance?" Logan placed his hand on her bare back as he led her to the dance floor. They danced to the next three songs and then decided they needed something to drink.

"What would you like," Logan asked.

"I would love some sparkling water. Thanks." He left her standing near the corner while he got their drinks. She was admiring how sweet he was, when she heard her name.

She looked up to see Duke towering over her. "You made it out tonight I see," his tone was playful with a hint of disdain. "Where's Kate this evening? Did you leave her home alone?"

She shook her head, "What is wrong with you? Do you really think I'd leave Kate alone tonight? She's with Abby at a church function for the night."

He looked smug, as if he knew she wouldn't leave Kate by herself at night, but he'd made her react. He smirked as if he'd won something and then changed the subject. "Are you enjoying yourself?"

"Yes, the Covingtons have outdone themselves. I'm glad I didn't miss it," Savanna reclaimed her composure.

"I see you have a date tonight," he said in a tone that took the conversation in an uncomfortable direction.

"Yes, he's a friend of Rachel and Bear's." She braced herself for the insult she knew was coming.

"Lucky guy." He continued to glare at her. "How much did you pay him?" Another self-satisfied smile crossed his face to match his mocking tone. "Did you bribe him to escort you, like you did my brother?"

She instantly knew that in innocence, Kate had told him about how she had traded her babysitting for his brother to escort her to Rachel's wedding.

She exhaled as she took the sting of his words. Her small but humiliating secret was out. Duke could ridicule her for her lack of dates, but she still had Kate. The realization of that jolted her confidence, and before she could control her mouth, she said, "Maybe I can't get a date—but at least I have guardianship of Kate." She pronounced Kate's name with an emphasis on the "T" for theatrics.

She had wiped the arrogance off his face with her reply, but she had an anxious inkling that she had just awoken a lion.

"Ms. St. James, would you do me the honors," he said, as he motioned toward the dance-floor. Duke was holding out his hand for her to take it and she was about to take pleasure in declining his offer.

"No, I don't—" he grabbed her hand and pulled her toward the dance floor before she could finish her answer. His long stride made it difficult to keep up in her high heels. He put his hand on the small of her bare back and led her onto the dance floor. To her dismay, the music had changed to Etta James's *At Last*. He pulled her close to him with one hand on the small of her back and held her other hand in his. She hadn't been this close in his proximity before—at least while she was conscious.

Her senses were overloaded with his scent and his arm around her. Words failed her. *"I can't think of a single cutting thing to say,"* she thought. All she could do was enjoy the dance. The world was fading away, and it was just the two of them. Stormy dark blue eyes gazed into blue-green ones. He leaned his head down on her forehead and she closed her eyes. The only thing that brought them back to reality was the crowd applauding the band. He let go of her abruptly and left her standing there. His actions confused her. One minute he was holding her close and the next, he had discarded her. In a daze, she scoured the ballroom for Logan.

The wait staff was passing out New Year's party favors and hats for the guests when she spotted her date talking to a woman on the other side of the room. He seemed to be deep in conversation with the woman, but she didn't care. Savanna's thoughts were so scattered, she wasn't sure which end-was-up. Someone placed a New Year's tiara on her head and handed her a rolled up noise maker.

Rachel was dancing with an elderly gentleman and Bear reached out to snag Savanna for a dance just as she was about to make an escape to the ladies room.

When Bear turned to talk to another guest, she made her way to the restroom and was thankful for the cool air and quietness when the door closed behind her.

She finished freshening her make-up and washing her hands, when she heard, "Hi, I'm Ashley Oliver," she held out her hand to shake Savanna's. The nurse part of Savanna was hoping that Ashley Oliver had already washed her hands since they were in the restroom.

"Hello—Savanna St. James," she said, as she shook Ashley's hand.

"Oh, yes—I know who *you* are. You're Kate's new guardian." Cattiness was in her tone.

"Yes, that's right, how do you know that?" Savanna looked down at the attractive dark-haired woman in front of her.

"I'm Duke's fiancé," she said with arrogance and held up her left hand to showcase the sparkling diamond ring. Savanna's heart sank, but she smiled at the other woman.

"Oh, that's—great. Best wishes!" With every cell in her body, she tried to make it sound as authentic as possible, to hide her discomfort.

"You know, I saw the two of you dancing together just now, and you looked very—intimate. I thought I would warn you, he's already taken," she said as she turned to reapply her red lipstick. "Keep your distance from Duke, because I'm a person with connections, and I won't mind finding out any information I can to help Duke gain rightful custody of his niece. I think we both know that you were only after Cash's wealth, and now Kate serves as an opportunity for you to get close to Duke. I suppose either of the Hollingsworth brothers will suffice—am I right?" She looked at Savanna in the mirror while she applied her lipstick.

As the shock of that conversation hit her, Savanna controlled her urge to fire back at the beautiful, but vile person standing before her. Ashley kept her eyes on Savanna.

"I haven't informed Duke yet, but I know all about your short-lived previous marriage. I have it on authority that you became violent and stabbed your ex-husband. I saw the police report. Lucky for you, he didn't press charges. You took the expensive jewelry and cash and left him with nothing."

Savanna's mouth was gaping open at the information. "Why would you be trying to find out information on me?" She was shaking on the inside that Creed had filed a police report on her after he had battered her and killed her dog.

Ashley laughed at her. "You didn't really think Duke is just going to hand Kate over to you so easily? Trust me, since I have a network of resources, I can bury you. I'm Duke's weapon against gold-diggers like you. Stay away from my fiancé or you will have hell to pay. Or worse, you'll lose Kate and then have no way to get your hands on any of Cash's money."

Savanna felt that Ashley's accusation didn't deserve a reaction. "I'll keep that in mind," she said and walked out the door to rejoin the party.

She grabbed a glass of champagne from a server's tray and chugged a large gulp before surging into the crowd to get on with the night's celebration. She hoped to forget the nightmare in the bathroom.

She and Logan had mingled and danced throughout the night. Her New Year's tiara was still on her head when the countdown started.

FIVE…. FOUR… THREE… TWO… ONE…. HAPPY NEW YEAR! Auld Lang Syne drifted through the ballroom full of revelers. Logan was standing by her and gave her a chaste peck on the forehead at midnight and then really kissed the other woman he had been in deep conversation with throughout the evening, but Savanna still didn't care.

She hugged Rachel and Bear as they moved around the crowd, wishing everyone a Happy New Year. Confetti continued to fall from the ceiling like colorful snow as another male stranger hugged her close.

A large hand grabbed hers and pulled her to the side and away from the crowd. It surprised her to find Duke smiling down at her as he stood there, and a snow of confetti littered his hair. "Don't I get a New Year's kiss?"

Before she could think, he grasped the back of her head. His mouth was on hers and he lost her for a few seconds in a soul-shattering kiss. Tongue and lips meshed together. Both of them were breathless as he pulled away. His dark blue eyes held hers. The unpleasant vision of Ashley Oliver, his fiancé, seeped into her mind. She pushed at his chest and broke free of his grip.

"What are you doing? You will stop at nothing to get Kate! You and your vile fiancé are insane!"

Savanna turned to escape his presence and ran into an elderly couple, almost knocking them over. "I'm so sorry," she told them. Her shoe fell off in the crowd, and to keep moving, she never looked for it. She hopped as she pulled off the other one and ran to find Logan. Savanna spotted him in the crowd and pleaded with him to take her home. After a few more words with the other woman, he guided her to the door.

A few minutes into the drive, Logan spoke, "I have to confess something."

Savanna looked at him, puzzled. "Ok?"

He glanced at her while driving, "I only agreed to take you to this New Year's Eve party because I knew my ex-wife would be there and I wanted to make her jealous enough to take me back, and it worked—she wants me back! I was talking to her most of the evening."

Savanna chuckled at the way the evening had ended, and the New Year began.

"Did I say something funny?" Her laughter perplexed him.

The humor of the situation reached a crescendo and tears rolled down her cheeks as she laughed. He chuckled as he witnessed her laughter. After she regained control of herself, she apologized for the temporary insanity.

"Logan—no worries about using me to get your ex back," she reassured him. "I enjoyed most of the evening and wouldn't have been able to go if you hadn't agreed to take me. Besides, you're just a few years too young for me. It's just... I helped facilitate you and your ex reconciling, and a woman warned me to stay away from her fiancé, all in the span of a few hours. To add insult to the evening, I lost my shoe and almost knocked over an elderly couple." She held up only one shoe. "And somewhere out there is my other shoe," she said with a sad face before laughing again. This time he was laughing with her.

"Savanna girl—you know how to start off a new year. Your cousin fixed me up with a dang wrecking ball," Logan teased. They both cracked up again, partly because of lack of sleep and due to the bizarre turn of events.

When they arrived at her house she told him, "Good luck to you on getting back with your ex," and shot a warm smile in his direction.

"I'm about to drive over to her place. Thanks again Savanna, and good luck to you too. Whoever gets you will be one lucky guy. If things don't work out with my ex, maybe we can be together."

"Right," she said with sarcasm and waved goodbye. "Thanks again for the flowers, they're my favorite."

He smiled and said goodnight, and she watched his taillights grow smaller in the distance.

~Chapter 18~

January was a mix of bitter cold days and milder days with sunshine. Duke picked Kate up from school a few times to allow her to see her colt Jesse as much as possible. Ashley Oliver had visited the ranch and the three of them went horseback riding in the evening until dark.

Savanna hid her dissatisfaction when Kate told her Ashley had offered to take her shopping and to a spa day.

She smiled and replied, "That sounds like a fun time."

She wasn't sure if she hated the fact that Duke was engaged to a battle ax or if she just hated that he was engaged. She tried her best to keep him out of her thoughts and avoid him as much as possible. She had the feeling that Ashley's threats weren't hollow, and she had no clue what Duke's intentions were at this point.

The worst thing was seeing Duke drive the three of them around in Ashley's Mercedes. Savanna had been waiting for Kate to get home from Duke's one afternoon when she looked out the window to see the three of them in Ashley's car—like a little family. "Ugh, that makes me want to vomit," she said aloud.

The only conclusion she could reach was that Duke must be just like Ashley. *"If only Kate didn't have to be around those two… but Duke is her family,"* she thought with anguish.

~Chapter 19~

Since it was Valentine's Day, she bought Kate some chocolates and some silver hoop earrings which she placed in a white gift bag with pink tissue paper, complete with a Valentine's Day card. Kate came bouncing in the door excited about the Valentine's Day dance which was from six to nine p.m. in the gymnasium.

She walked into the kitchen and spotted her gift bag from Savanna. "Can I open it," she shrieked as she opened the jewelry box. "Oh. My. Gosh. I love them! Thank you, Savanna."

The doorbell rang and Savanna slid to the door in her socks to see a flower delivery guy standing there with two bouquets of flowers and a balloon. One bouquet had three white and three red roses along with a balloon that said: Happy Valentine's Day!

The other bouquet was two dozen pink Ranunculus, which were breathtaking. She thanked him and carried them into the house. Kate was reading the card on the bouquet with the balloon. "It's from Uncle Duke. How sweet!"

Kate eyed the other mammoth display of flowers, "What does the card say?"

Savanna pulled open the small envelope and read the card.

TO MY DEAREST SAVANNA:

HAPPY VALENTINE'S DAY. I'M SO HAPPY I FOUND YOU! SEE YOU SOON.

"Do you know who sent them?"

"No—no clue, but I do love pink Ranunculus." A smile lit Savanna's face as she sniffed the flowers and placed them in the middle of the table. Kate was admiring her own balloon and bouquet from her Uncle Duke.

"Kate, you'd better get ready, your Uncle Duke will be by to drop you off at the dance in an hour and a half."

Duke showed up looking handsome as usual. Kate let him in the house and as he walked into the kitchen, he saw the bouquet and balloon he had sent to Kate. "Did you like them?"

"They're beautiful, Uncle Duke, thank you!" She hugged him.

"Happy Valentine's Day, Kiddo."

"Wow, your teen boyfriend must have spent a year's worth of weekly allowance on that epic display of Ranunculus," he said to Kate, while observing the flower arrangement on the table.

She rolled her eyes. "First, Uncle Duke, I don't have a boyfriend yet, and second, they're not for me. They're Savanna's from an unknown person—see." She handed him the card and crossed her arms. Duke read the card and then placed it back in the envelope.

"Interesting."

Savanna walked into the kitchen and saw the two of them standing there. Kate was dressed for the dance. "You look gorgeous, Kate! I love the outfit." Kate twirled around in dramatic fashion to model.

"Do you think my eye make-up looks on-point?"

"Girl—you know it does," Savanna drawled.

Duke shook his head. "Women."

"You'd better get going or you might be fashionably late," Savanna warned.

Duke gave her a lingering look before walking out the door behind Kate. "Someone must really be into you—two dozen pink Ranunculus from a secret admirer. Impressive."

Savanna shrugged and said, "Surprised?" It was the only comeback she could think of before she closed the door behind him. His presence seemed to decrease the neurons firing in her brain.

~Chapter 20~

~Duke~

Being with his niece the last few months and experiencing life with her, made him think about what he had been missing out on his entire life. His mother used to say, "Duke Darling, I'm not getting any younger and I have only one grandchild to brag about. You're wrecking my bragging rights in my social circle. How am I to fit in at the club?"

He relished those moments seeing his niece ride horses and care for Jesse, or the moments when she performed cheer routines in front of a middle school crowd, or performed in band concerts. He had watched her mature so much in the last five months. She watched football with him and had even accompanied him to cattle auctions. Her laugh was infectious, although her attitude and eye rolls could test the patience of a saint. He didn't even mind the occasional hormonal meltdowns typical for a thirteen-year-old girl.

Savanna... he thought. She had appeared into his life out of nowhere—standing there with his niece in Leland Owen's office. How the heck did she end up intertwined so deep in Cash's life? How did she make such an impression on his brother that he would have left her his most valuable asset—Kate, instead of giving guardianship to his own brother? Was she really after Cash's wealth? He cursed the fact that he found it hard not to stare when she was in his vicinity. He kept her at a distance to observe how she lived her life and to see how she treated Kate. Her affection for his niece seemed to be authentic, and Kate—it seemed Savanna was like a mother to her. He didn't want to disrupt any stability his niece had gained over the last few months by removing Savanna out of her life. As they had taught him in the military... he'd observe and gather information for a while and then take the required action.

Thoughts of his brother drifted into his mind. Cash—the guy who flew by the seat of his pants, even as a kid—was always impulsive and reckless. During his grade school years, he had been a daredevil and got into fights at school. His father was a colonel in the military and couldn't identify with his lack of discipline. They had gotten into many heated arguments. Their mother adored Cash, though. He was her baby. She catered to him more than she did Duke since Duke was their father's favorite. He was more studious, disciplined, and watched out for Cash during their childhood.

They would tease each other without mercy. Cash would call him Dooky- Head instead of Duke, or Duke- Makes- Me- Puke.

Duke could outsmart him at every game they played. They would bet their allowance on every game whether it was a game of basketball or Monopoly, and Duke won every time. He had a nice stash of money one summer because of his haul from the bets, but despite their sibling rivalry, Duke loved his younger brother.

After Cash graduated high school, he joined the Army for discipline and to please his father. It shocked his family when they found out he was engaged to Amy. He had never given the impression that he would ever settle down with just one woman, but when he met Amy, he had eyes for no other. She was his obsession.

Then, Kate was born. Cash adored her, and when Amy died, he did his best to give her a stable life. Duke admired him for that, because he knew it couldn't be easy doing it alone.

Cash had never dated after that, but had an unhealthy preoccupation with avenging Amy's death. His impulsive attributes resurfaced, and he had vowed to remove Amy's killer from society. In error, Duke thought his brother had made peace that he would never find who murdered his wife. Then Savanna entered his life, and allowed him to pull one last irresponsible and fatal stunt. Duke shook his head, confounded by the whole situation.

His uncontrollable urge to kiss Savanna at the New Year's party stunned him. That kiss had revisited his mind more than he liked. Even worse, he couldn't bring himself to feel remorse, even though he's engaged to Ashley. His controlled world was becoming unraveled in every direction since Savanna St. James entered his life, but he intended to put things back in order and soon—whatever it took.

Ashley discouraged him from spending much time with Savanna—the-gold-digger—as she called her. He usually had an accurate intuition about people, and Savanna didn't give him the impression that she was after his brother's money or status. She almost seemed to isolate herself from society. Her house was in the middle of almost ten acres with no neighbors, and she had her own home.

A smile breached his lips as he knew firsthand that she had weapons to defend herself. He ran his hand through his hair and laughed about that night she'd almost shot him at close range. Was she afraid of someone or something? It had been five months since she came into his life, but he still didn't know any of her history other than when she met up with his younger brother, an old friend at the hardware store. She always avoided talking about herself and seemed to dodge his presence as much as possible.

~Kate's Thirteenth Birthday Party~

Kate's thirteenth birthday, March eighteenth, was as special as they could make it—considering it was the first one without her dad. Ashley was in South Carolina at her law firm and couldn't be there for Kate's birthday party. She invited three of her closest friends from church and school for a sleepover. Kate had picked out her own cake design and all the decorations. They also went to a trampoline park earlier in the day.

Savanna had gone out to get a few more things for the party while Duke stayed at the house to chaperon the girls. She returned home to Duke and a house full of teenagers. The girls were occupying the living room while watching a movie. As much as she didn't relish being alone with Duke, she thought maybe it would be safe to sit out on the back porch and have iced tea with him while the girls watched a movie.

He opened the door for her as she carried a wooden handled tray with tea for the both of them. It was slightly chilly outside, but the fresh air was magnificent and relaxing. While sipping their drinks, they gazed out at the pasture behind the house.

"This is nice." He leaned back in his chair and relaxed.

Savanna's soft laugh filled the silence. "Yeah, it's a quiet break from the noise inside."

"I meant, you've got a peaceful place out here on this acreage." A soft wind moved the trees as he glanced at her.

"I knew I wanted to live in the middle of a patch of land, so I had this house built two years ago when I got out of the Air Force."

"You mentioned that the scar on your left arm was from your days in the military. What happened?"

It surprised Savanna that he had remembered her scar. "I was a registered nurse stationed at Ramstein Air Force Base in Germany. We would sometimes fly to Bagram Air Base in Afghanistan to pick up wounded soldiers and bring them back to Landstuhl Regional Medical Center in Germany. Our team was flying on a C-17 aircraft to intercept some wounded soldiers and we would always land at Bagram without lights for tactical reasons. It had become routine, and there had been no problems. Until one night, as my unit was loading a patient onto the aircraft, we heard an explosion. I felt a searing, burning pain on my left arm but continued to get our wounded soldier patient out of harm's way. I looked down at my uniform, which was saturated with blood and didn't know if it was mine or someone else's. Then I realized that something had ripped my uniform open, and I had a gaping wound. A metal piece being hurled at us during the explosion, sliced from my shoulder to my forearm. I received many stitches and physical therapy. I've also seen a few plastic surgeons since then, and it looks much better than it did in the beginning. Loud noises still bother me to this day — takes me back to that horrifying moment." She looked at him when she finished.

"We have that in common."

"The scar or the loud noises?"

"Both." He grinned.

"I'm sorry to hear that. Cash said you were in the Navy." She took a sip of her drink.

"I was a Navy SEAL and was in my element. I'd always been one to protect and rescue from an early age, since Cash was always getting himself into precarious situations with fights and mischief." He grinned at recalling that bit of information.

"I went on a few missions into enemy infested territory in which I wasn't exactly sure I'd return home. We rescued a few missionaries in Africa and went on multiple missions in the Middle East. I lost a few comrades along the way—that's been hard, but I wouldn't change my career choice for the world. If I had died over there, I would have died with my weapon and boots on, doing what God put me on this earth to do."

She looked at him and admired his valor and that he had pursued his purpose. "I'm sure you've made a difference because of your career choice. The world owes you a debt of gratitude." Savanna's reply was heartfelt.

"I can say the same for you." He smiled at her.

"How did you meet my brother in the beginning?"

When the Air Force stationed me in Germany, they assigned Cash to my intensive care unit after he had sustained abdominal trauma and had emergency surgery to correct the internal bleeding from the impact. Because of the blood loss and his need for pain control, I spent a lot of time at his bedside. He'd share a few stories about how he'd always beat you at basketball or at chess and win money from you every single time. I also know that he loved to call you Ol' Dooky-Head." Duke laughed out loud that Cash had told her that, and Savanna continued with her story.

"We found out we were both from Georgia—and grew up about an hour's drive from each other. He told me he couldn't wait to marry Amy when he got back to the states and he even wanted me to meet her someday. Cupid had smitten him with love for her. We made a lifelong connection in that ICU. I remember feeling so sad to see him go and hoped that he got to marry Amy when he returned to the states. One of the last things he had said before they flew him to the states was that maybe we could all meet in Georgia someday, including his older brother." She glanced over at Duke to note his reaction. He gave a deep laugh and shook his head.

"That sounds like something he'd say and you're right, Amy consumed him." Duke raised his brows. "Cash was also a big-fat liar. He never won at anything he challenged me to. I was rich every summer after all the bets he lost."

Savanna's face was alight with laughter. "How could he lie to me like that?"

"Did you have a nickname for *him*," she asked.

"I called him *Dough-Boy* since people refer to cash as dough, and he hated it, which made me call him that even more. I've gotta give him credit though. He might have been a dough-boy, but he never backed down from a challenge. He'd keep trying, just like he did after Amy's death. You must have known about his obsession with repaying her killers," he said.

"I sensed his bitterness toward them and knew someday he'd serve them justice in one form or another. When I found him in Stillwell County, he was already planning."

"Is that when you told him you would keep Kate?"

"Yes, a few weeks after we had reconnected," she blushed, knowing that he was also recalling that she had asked his brother to be her date in return, and looked away from his gaze. He smiled at her embarrassment and she was wishing she could let it go.

Savanna segwayed the subject to him. "You've asked me about my relationship status before, but I'm afraid I know little about yours." She pushed some blonde strands out of her face as the soothing breeze mussed her hair.

He studied her for a moment, taken aback by her boldness.

"How long have you been engaged to Ashley?" She queried.

"We got engaged in June last year and plan to marry in the fall of this year."

"No wedding date yet?"

"Not... yet."

"Fascinating. What's the holdup?" She was enjoying the possibility of his discomfort for once.

"Ashley is a partner in a law firm in South Carolina and works many hours along with her frequent international travels. After Cash died, and after I inherited his property,

I've been busy here in Stillwell County getting the house finished and maintaining the land and livestock—and then there's Kate."

He looked at her. "When Cash died, it changed everything. I have to make sure that Ashley and Kate get along—they will eventually belong in the same family."

Savanna swallowed hard at that statement. Ashley was the last person who should get to belong in the Hollingsworth family, but she kept that thought to herself.

Duke served the cross-examination right back at her. "How long were *you* married?" She looked up, unprepared for his question.

"Almost a year," she said, and then didn't offer any further information.

He raised his brows as if the length of her marriage surprised him, and his mouth opened to probe the subject further when Kate opened the back door.

"Savanna, can you help me with this remote, I can't get the movie to resume!" Kate was tapping the remote on the door frame as she spoke.

Savanna got up from her chair on the back porch, relieved that Kate saved her once more. She didn't want to go into any detail about her brief but horrifying and abusive marriage to Creed Kelley. It probably wouldn't help Duke's opinion of her either, as he would probably think she couldn't make good life choices in picking a husband. She assumed Ashley hadn't filled him in on her past.

"Excuse me for a moment," she said as she passed by him.

After Savanna left him on the back porch, he reflected on all he had learned about her in the past hour and decided that he'd have to find another opportunity to learn more. Her mystery intrigued him. "This is getting frustrating," he said as he ran his hands through his hair.

~Chapter 21~

Savanna wanted a barbed wire fence lining her property and placed a few fence posts last summer. A barbed wire fence would keep trespassers out, and maybe someday she'd get a couple horses, although she knew little about how to care for them. She smiled at her pipe dream.

Before she had started the project, sweet Mr. Perkins who owned the hardware store had driven all the way out to her place to show her how to use her new power auger to dig the post holes. After a day of sore muscles she never knew existed, she developed her skills boring holes in the ground. He taught her to put gravel a few inches down in the hole to keep the posts from staying wet at the bottom. She had her cement and buckets of water. It was a process, and she had taken her time to do it the right way.

He showed her a trick to setting the cement around the poles at ground level. "Now sugar, you wanna slope that cement so that water always drains away from the pole after a rain." She demonstrated the skills he taught her and his eyes lit up, "You're a dern fast learner, Savannie. You could lay fence posts with the best of em." Her face was glowing with pride at his praise. She cherished that day. Ellis Perkins had shown her a valuable skill. It would have been out of her price range to hire someone to do it, and it was just more fun being outdoors doing it herself, anyway.

She decided that today was as good a day to place more posts in the ground. It was windy and chilly out, but the sun was shining. A few dark clouds hung in the distance.

Kate went to the mall with a few of her friends, and this was the perfect opportunity to make progress on her project. She threw on a black turtleneck, athletic shirt for warmth along with black leggings and work boots. Before she left the house, her reflection looked more like a ninja than a fence layer. Her blonde hair was in a large heap on top of her head with a lavender headband covering her ears while loads of Chap Stick coated her lips to protect them from the wind.

The post holes had been coming along nicely, but holding the auger was making her back stiff. She stopped working long enough to stand up straight and stretch her lower back. Her hands rested on her hips as she held her work gloves in one hand.

"Make sure you line them up straight." A deep voice came from out of nowhere. Duke was walking toward her.

"Yeah, I'll keep that in mind," she said with a smirk, surprised that he was there. "What are you doing all the way out here?" She questioned in a pleasant tone as he moved closer.

"Came to see Kate, but I saw you out here and figured she'd gone somewhere for the day. Could you use some help?"

A slow smile spread across her lips and his eyes held hers as if he were drinking in her smile. "You know how to operate a power auger," she asked with playfulness.

He gave a single curt nod in response. "Let me get some work gloves out of my truck."

She watched his long stride as he walked the short distance back to his truck parked along the road. It was getting harder to detach her feelings for him as he returned toward her, slipping on his gloves. Usually, she was too proud to accept much help, but she sure as heck wouldn't turn it down today. Her back and arms had been through the paces.

Time passed, and they worked without saying much. He would stop to wipe his brow and watch her pour gravel into the bottom half of the hole he dug. He admired her skill and wondered where she'd learned to lay fence posts. He laughed to himself. Her mountain of hair bobbed forward and backward as she worked. *"It's freakin' hilarious yet adorable."* He shook his head at his obtuse thoughts. *"What has happened to my brain?"*

She continued to work without looking up, as if lost in her own world. Thunder approached in the near distance and they looked up to see some lightning highlighting the deep gray clouds. Without warning, sprinkles cascaded down on them. Duke grabbed the auger and covered the power tool with a tarp in the back of his truck. She grabbed her bag of cement and ran for the truck. He took the bag from her and slid it under the tarp with the auger. Rain was picking up and the smell of freshness filled the air.

"Get in." He motioned for her to get in the truck. She almost slipped in mud in her haste to step up into the cab and caught herself on the door as she climbed in. He laughed, "Nice recovery," he said as he held the door for her.

"Shut up," she shot back with a grin.

The rain was drumming on the hood as he got in on the driver's side. "I think the weather has canceled our fence post placement for the day," she said and looked over at him. "Hey, thanks for helping me. The work goes faster with two."

"I had fun."

"Right." She laughed. "It's such an exciting life out here in the middle of nowhere, laying fence posts and all."

He turned, facing her. "So, I would like to know why you wanted to be out here in the middle of nowhere—alone."

"I was looking for a peaceful place…. you know… in the middle of a grassy pasture, surrounded by trees… a place I can watch the sunset from my back porch." She looked as though she were picturing it in her mind.

"Since your divorce, have there been any relationships since moving out here?"

"Careful Savanna, he's probably fishing for Intel to find anything to hold against you, just like he did at Kate's party."

"No. Glenn Oaks isn't exactly a dating mecca. Besides, I have everything I need out here and now I have Kate." She tried to punt it away.

"Don't you get lonely?" He kept the subject on track.

"I might ask you the same thing," she countered.

"I have Ashley."

"I bet your relationship is great from a few hundred miles away." She laid some sass into her statement as his questioning of her lack of relationship irritated her. "I'm sorry, I shouldn't—have," guilt spread through her, then her apology to him irritated her even more.

He smirked at her wit. "No, it's okay. I guess to most people, our distance might seem cold, but it works for us. I guess I'm puzzled that someone like you is single and isolated. It makes me wonder what happened to you." He stared out the windshield and then looked over at her as he finished his statement.

She shrugged, "I suppose I'm not a people person, or maybe I just seem odd to most men. I'm also in my forties and I don't know if you've heard, but the dating world holds little value for women in their forties. Our sexual market value is allegedly zero, but men my age can get women much younger than they are. Apparently, being established, looking distinguished and having lasting virility helps maintain your value."

She was on a roll and kept going. "I guess I could ask the same to someone who looks like Don Draper, has a fiancé in another state, and doesn't spend Christmas with her or have a wedding date set. What happened to you?"

"Touché." He said then smiled. "You think I look like Don Draper?"

She shrugged to appear indifferent.

"I'm also glad you educated me on my sexual market value. Evidently, I have it a lot better than you do." Her face flushed, betraying her again. They sat in silence and listened to the rain for a few moments.

"I have extra bottled water and beef jerky... want some," he offered.

"Mmm that sounds good, I'm starving." The rain continued to pour as they sat there.

He handed her a package of jerky and pulled out a bottle from a small insulated bag. Her hand brushed his as she took the bottle. Dark blue eyes met hers as she felt the electricity between them. *"Act normal Savanna... jeez. Get it together."*

Instead of driving back to the house, they sat and ate their jerky and sipped on water as if they were at a picnic while they waited for the rain to let up.

"What is something you've never seen that you want to see someday," he asked.

She swallowed the jerky and took a drink. "Well—I've always wanted to see the Northern Lights in Finland."

He smiled at her as he took in her answer. "That would be something... I've never seen it either."

"What about you... what would you want to see?"

He looked over at her. "I—would like to see a cattle drive.... you know... just horses... chuck wagon for meals.... all those cattle, while wearing a cowboy hat." He listed them off.

Her laugh was a melody to his ears. "I could totally see you doing that. You would probably look stunning in a cowboy hat." She tilted her head to picture him wearing one.

"Trust me... I look stunning in my cowboy hat." His humor made her forget they were enemies for a moment. Their light bantering was soothing. "I wear one, now that I've taken over Cash's ranch... all those horses and cattle. It's a sight to see sometimes first thing in the morning."

"I'll bet it is. I can envision my fields with a couple horses someday. That's kinda one reason I wanted this fence." She gestured toward her pasture.

"I hope you get your dream someday then." He gave her a brief glance.

She removed her lavender headband since they were out of the wind and a few strands had fallen from the blonde tower piled on top of her head. He reached over to grasp a strand between his thumb and forefinger and ran his fingers to the end and let it go. She stiffened. "You had a piece of fuzz," he said and trained his eyes on her.

She felt the need to break the spell and hurried to ask him a question.

"Do you miss your career?"

He paused before answering. "Yeah—every day. I miss the brotherhood and the challenges. My aches and pains with the weather is a souvenir of the better part of my life." Sarcasm accompanied his smile.

"I would imagine acclimating back into civilian life was difficult. Was it hard for you?" Her voice was soft. He looked at her for a moment and answered. "I was in a depressed state when I returned home. My family tried to help, but I had shut everyone out to deal with the darkness." His breath caught in his chest as she rested her hand on his shoulder for a second. "That sucks… sorry you went through that," she said as she realized what she had done and jerked her hand from his shoulder. His hand caught hers midway down and their joined hands rested on the console. *"Just breathe Savanna…. he does not have feelings for you, he's just being friendly to get your guard down…. stop panicking and try to act normal."*

The rain stopped, and she took that opportunity to lighten the mood. She pulled her hand out of his. "I better get things put away. Doesn't look like there will be anymore fence post placement today." He stared at her as if he were trying to figure out what was going on in her head, which made her even more uncomfortable. He leaned back with a self-satisfied smile while she grabbed the door handle and climbed out. He met her at the back of the truck to get the auger and cement. They loaded all her equipment into her mid-sized ATV. The ground sloshed beneath their feet as they worked.

"Hey, thanks again for the help, Duke. I appreciate it." He looked at her mouth as she spoke and stepped closer. She wasn't sure what his intentions were, but she decided not to stand there and find out.

She brushed the damp seat off with her sleeve and reached for the key in her pocket. Then, sat down behind the wheel with him standing near her.

"Tell Kate I'll come by to see her some time," he said.

"I will," she shouted over the engine as she nodded and waved. She drove toward the house while praying that she didn't get stuck in the mud. She saw the brake lights on Duke's truck from the corner of her eye and knew he was leaving. A part of her wished he would have stayed longer and another part of her couldn't breathe just thinking about it.

~Chapter 22~

As the trees budded, and the flowers bloomed, Kate was already making plans for summer. She and Savanna had gone through brochures of summer camps and she planned to go with her best friend, Abby. Booking in April ensured a reservation at summer camp. Camp Kawkanuk was the coveted summer destination for early teens, and the two of them had decided that this was the one for summer. The whole month of June she'd spend camping, canoeing, eating S'mores, and swimming with her best friend. She was face-timing Abby while booking, to ensure they got the same camp. Shrieks of delight rattled Savanna's eardrums as both the girls celebrated their confirmed summer plans over the phone.

Later in the evening, Savanna dried off and wrapped a towel around her after a relaxing shower. She wrapped her hair in a towel and piled it atop her head. Then she heard Kate answering the doorbell and threw on a robe.

Kate was looking for a card in the two-dozen pink Ranunculus arrangement. "They're for you, Savanna!" Kate handed her an envelope with SAVANNA written on the front. The card said:

MY DEAREST SAVANNA

I CAN'T WAIT TO SEE YOU THIS SUMMER, NOW THAT I FOUND YOU.

I'VE DECIDED THAT YOU BELONG WITH ME.

I HAVE GREAT PLANS FOR YOU.

ENJOY THE PINK RANUNCULUS.

SEE YOU SOON

Savanna looked up from the card. "Kate, who delivered the flowers?"

Kate shrugged, "Someone in—like—a ball cap and sunglasses, why?"

Savanna ignored her question. "What did they look like? Male or Female?"

"Uh—I didn't pay attention. The flower arrangement is like—huge. The person was taller than me with—like—medium colored skin, I guess. I'm not sure what kind of hair. Sorry—I didn't pay much attention." She shrugged again.

"No worries, Kate." She tried to keep her voice calm, but she had an alarming feeling in her gut. The flower deliveries were creeping her out—and the note… had Logan decided that she belonged with him? She had dismissed the flowers on Valentine's Day since she had been busy and forgot about them.

Of the few online dates she had gone on in the last few years, she couldn't think of anyone who would have been trying to reconnect. Most were decent, normal guys. There were a few weirdos. Like, the guy who lived with his mother, and his Momma would call him every thirty minutes while he was on a date. Then, she remembered the bald one who wanted to get married after only a week of talking to her online, and when she rejected him, he asked her for a small lock of her hair to remember their time together. She shuddered. She wished she hadn't filled out the, "My Favorite Things" section of the online dating profile. She couldn't recall, but maybe she had mentioned her love for pink Ranunculus. *"Ugh, I so regret the whole online dating phase of my life,"* she lamented to herself.

To figure it out, she called the flower shop that had delivered her flowers on Valentine's Day.

"Flower Power—this is Pam—how may I help you?"

"Hi Pam—this is Savanna St. James, and I received a bouquet of twenty-four pink Ranunculus. I was wondering if you'd be able to tell me who might have sent them."

She heard Pam talking to someone in the background. "Savanna, honey, we have delivered no pink Ranunculus this week." Savanna thanked her and ended the call. She spent the next half-hour calling around to the only other two florists who would have delivered in her area, but with no luck.

~Chapter 23~

It was the last day of seventh grade, and she saw Kate ambling from the bus for the last time that school year.

Kate bounded in the front door, "Woohooooo! I completed seventh grade!" Savanna high-fived her and took part in her celebration as they danced around the living room. "Let the summer fun begin! Only three days until Camp Kawkanuk. I'm gonna start packin' today," Kate announced.

"Jeez Kate, I think we've packed everything-but-the-washer and dryer." She had two suitcases and a backpack. The plan was that Kate would ride with Abby's parents to camp in east Tennessee.

Duke offered to drive Savanna to drop off Kate and say their goodbyes. He pulled up in his truck and loaded the suitcases. "Girl, just how much stuff do you need for camp? There's enough stuff here for three people," he teased.

Kate gave him a look with attitude. "Uncle Duke, you don't get it—I'm leaving for an entire month.... a girl needs different clothes and shoes."

"If you say so, Squirt," he said with dry humor.

They made it to Abby's house and watched Kate get into the passenger van. Savanna couldn't help the lump in her throat as they waved goodbye. It was the first time away from Kate in six months. "It's going to be awfully quiet around the house." She said in a quiet tone. She and Duke walked back to the truck and headed for home.

"You mind if we roll the windows down?" Duke glanced sideways at Savanna.

She grinned, "I like your style." They rolled the windows down and Kenny Chesney was blasting out of the speakers. It was a carefree moment they both enjoyed—one that didn't require conversation—a moment of freedom. Open fields whizzed by and Savanna held her hand out to let the wind make waves of it. She forgot that she was riding with Duke until they slowed to a stop sign. She glimpsed at herself in the side mirror. Her hair was a windblown mess, but she didn't care.

"Hey, there's something I want to show you out at the ranch," he said.

"Uh—ok, sure."

He drove them out to his place, past the remarkable, almost completed new house, and on to the large barn on the acreage.

Duke led her into the barn, to a stall where a foal stood and opened the stall to let her in to pet it. "He's so soft!" His coat was coal black with a white streak down his face. "When was he born," she said with childlike excitement.

"Yesterday evening. We thought his mom was going to need help, but she gave birth on her own."

The foal was enjoying the attention. "Come on, I'll show you Kate's colt—Jesse." They walked together to another area with stalls and a beautiful brown colt came toward them. Savanna could tell he was used to attention from Kate. He bobbed his head as she spoke to him in baby talk.

"Wittle Desse—so coot." She rubbed his head.

"Wittle Desse? Keep that up, and he'll never learn to speak properly," Duke said with dry humor.

Laughter bubbled from her after hearing Duke pronounce Jesse's name that way.

"And this guy over here—Seth, is my gelding." Duke pointed to another shiny brown horse with a white streaked face.

"What's a gelding?"

"It's a castrated horse." He smirked and watched to see her reaction.

Her face reddened. "Oh—ouch."

"That's what *he* said!"

"Ha. Ha. That's why he has a long face." Savanna returned the trite joke and Duke laughed at her dorky humor.

"Why would you castrate him? Doesn't he need that—part," she asked with innocence.

Duke was trying not to laugh at her question. "He's a working horse and doesn't need hormone-induced aggression. We want him to remain calm."

"Want to ride him?" Duke took hold of the reins.

"I—I've never ridden a horse in my life," Savanna admitted.

"Never?" He gawked at her in disbelief. Then, led the horse out of the stall and into the sunlight.

"Come on," he motioned for her to come closer. "I'll help you up in the saddle."

Savanna pointed to the saddle, "You want me to get up there?"

"Um… yeah—that's how people usually ride horses," he said with sarcasm and chuckled at her trepidation.

"Ok, then...here goes." She put her left foot in the stirrup and Duke boosted her hips to allow her other foot to clear the saddle. "I can't believe I'm up here. What do I do—where's the brake and accelerator?"

"*You* can just sit up there and look pretty. I'll take the reins and lead Seth." He guided the horse along a beaten path.

A breeze was blowing her hair, and she wished she'd worn a hair tie.

He looked back at her. "You ok?"

She gave a thumbs up.

She couldn't remember feeling this happy… ever. There was something to this whole, *"Being out in nature with animals, thing."* Well—that, and Duke was being…

sweet to her, but he's engaged. *"Come back to reality, Savanna."*

He led them back to the barn and helped Savanna off the horse. His hand seemed to linger on her waist a little longer than necessary, but she thought she was imagining things. Duke put Seth back in his stall and Savanna waited while he finished with the other horses.

She looked a few feet away from her to see a yellow lab coming toward her. "Brodie," she breathed.

"What?" Duke looked confused and looked from her to the dog wagging his tail. She stood staring at the dog with her hand over her mouth for a moment and then bent down to pet him.

"Oh yeah, that boy's name is Zack. He loves chewing on shoes." Duke noted her reaction to his dog and thought it odd. "I guess you're a fan of dogs?"

"Uh—yeah, they're great companions." She smiled up at him while she petted the dog.

"Yeah, I agree, I had a therapy dog named Walker. He was a chocolate lab, but passed away a few years ago," he said and could have sworn he saw tears in her eyes.

"It's always tough when they die, kinda like a piece of you dies with them," she replied and then straightened and tried to calm herself after seeing Brodie's replica.

"You ready?"

The two of them got back in the truck for Duke to drive her home.

He pulled the massive truck into her driveway just as the sun was setting. "Thank you for taking us today and for letting me ride Seth. I had a great time." She put her fingers on the handle to open the truck door.

"I'll see you in," Duke said.

"No, that's ok, I can—you don—," before she could get her objection out of her mouth, he was already out of the truck, around to her side, helping her out. He walked up the walkway behind her. She opened the wrought iron screen door to discover a taped note with the letters SAVANNA. Someone wrote them the same as the flower envelope she had received in April. She tensed and tried to hide the note out of Duke's view, but she wasn't stealth enough. He spotted the note, but didn't ask questions.

She ripped the taped note off, unlocked the door, and Duke followed her inside.

"I'm sure you're probably thirsty. Can I get you something to drink?" He stood there and looked at her with his head tilted as if he were trying to put a piece of the puzzle together.

"I'll take water, thanks," he said in a dry tone.

She reached into the cabinet and pulled down two tall glasses and filled them with the cold filtered water from the fridge. He looked around the house as she worked. She placed his glass on the counter-top and took a swallow of her water.

"Thanks." He drank half the water and sat the glass down.

"Who is the note from, Savanna?"

"I don't know… I haven't opened it." She tried to sound aloof.

"Who would leave a note taped to your door… way out here in the middle of nowhere?"

"The neighbor?" She said it in a guessing tone, trying to sound cute.

"You don't have neighbors—open the note," he demanded.

"There's this thing called privacy, Duke." Her attitude was making a comeback, but something told her now was not the time to show it off.

He glared at her.

"Fine." She tried her best to open it with a steady hand because her insides were trembling with dread of what someone wrote inside, not to mention the man standing in her kitchen, demanding she open it in front of him.

Someone typed in block letters:

MY DEAREST SAVANNA

I HOPE YOU ENJOYED THE PINK RANUNCULUS LAST MONTH. IT DISAPPOINTED ME I DIDN'T SEE YOU BUT I'LL SEE YOU THIS SUMMER.

A CUTE LITTLE MAGPIE TOLD ME WHERE I MIGHT FIND YOU.

YOU BELONG TO ME.

SEE YOU SOON

She looked up at Duke to find him rubbing his beard scruff in an irritated manner.

"Is this the same anonymous person who delivered flowers to you on Valentine's?"

"Yes—I mean, I'm not sure because the same Flower Power company that delivered Kate's flowers also delivered my anonymous Valentine flowers."

"The flowers from last month—we don't know what the person looked like that delivered them. I — "

He interrupted her. "Wait… what do you mean—we. Has Kate seen this person," he demanded as he walked closer to her to tower over her.

The need to explain engulfed her. "Well… on the day I received the flowers, I was getting out of the shower when Kate answered the door. A man or woman handed her the enormous bouquet. She couldn't remember exactly what they looked like or the vehicle they drove." Duke was struggling to hold his temper in check and cursed under his breath.

"Have you filed a statement with Stillwell County," he asked, as if she were a moron.

"Yes, I have! I made a statement last month and took the notes along with the flowers. I'm not a moron," she said, hoping he would calm down.

"When the hell were you going to tell me about this, Savanna?" His palm slammed down on the counter-top as he yelled at her. She flinched as if he had hit her.

"I thought the problem had gone away. I had security cameras installed, and the Sheriff makes rounds out this way every day." She crossed her arms over her torso and rubbed the back of her arms.

He ran a hand through his hair. "Why would you keep that information from me?" He exhaled as if he had figured out her reason.

"You mean to tell me," he said with a flushed face and nostrils flaring, "You'd rather endanger Kate's life and keep her with you, then let her stay with her own flesh and blood?"

She hated the icy vibe he was giving her. She couldn't believe this was the same man who had been so kind to her at his ranch an hour before.

"I would never deliberately endanger Kate. I love her. She means the world to me."

"Maybe Ashley was right about you," he shot back.

Duke might as well have branded her with a hot iron as he had just scorched her with his words. His temper raged. "I let it slide when you threw it in my face that you had guardianship of Kate at the New Year's Eve party, but you're about to find out just how ruthless I can be," he said in an even, but lethal tone, stepping closer to her again.

She met his stare with defiance and straightened up to her full height. "People have pushed me around my entire life and I've fought back. I'll take you on, too," she said in a quiet and steady voice.

Savanna felt a fire igniting on the inside. She'd had enough. Her unexpected determination kept her calm and her eyes held his as if this was a fight she wouldn't back down from. "I think you should leave," she said while holding eye contact and pointed to the door.

Without a word, he brushed past her as he stormed out the door.

~Chapter 24~

Dirt stained her white tank top as she pulled weeds in the flower bed and placed new mulch. The weeds flew through the air as she pulled them. Her skin was pink from hours out in the sun. She had almost mowed the whole acreage on a riding mower. The hum of the mower, along with the mindless task, was calming. Not knowing what more to do after the menacing note left on her door, and after Duke's threat a few days prior, had frayed her nerves. She kept busy with her job or chores around the house as a distraction.

She saw the deputy coming up the drive and stopped digging in the dirt to wipe her hands on her pants as she stood. His car stirred up dust as he came to a stop in her driveway.

"Afternoon, Savanna," Deputy Dawson greeted her with an apologetic look on his face. "I hope you're doing ok out here. These papers are for you. He thrust the papers in her hand.

Sweat dripped down her face as she took the delivery from him with a questioning look. He tipped his hat to her. "Don't stay out in this heat too long, ma'am."

Savanna watched him leave her property and stood there with the papers he had handed her. Her dusty finger smudged one of white pages. She held her breath as she skimmed the words.

Court Summons---Edward Duke Hollingsworth—on behalf of (minor) Kate Vivienne Hollingsworth — June 10th @ 9am.

She sat down on some cement pavers and let the teardrops fall with her head resting in her hands. What she feared became a reality. Dirt caked to her face where the tears flowed.

~Chapter 25~

Leland Owens declined to take her case since he had been the family attorney for Cash and Duke. He thought it would be a conflict of interest, but recommended one of his trusted attorney colleagues. Savanna had no resentment for his position in the matter as she knew his previous dealings with the Hollingsworth family.

"I hope you understand my predicament, Savanna," he said.

"I do, Leland, and I'm grateful for the recommendation," she reassured him.

A few days later, Savanna was sitting in her office when it occurred to her that Kate may be in danger if she remained Kate's guardian. As much as it broke her heart, she knew she had to let Kate go. Cash and Brodie were sources of unconditional love in her life. Some evil person took them from her too.

"I don't know my own fate, and I haven't considered what this anonymous person has in store for me," she thought with a heavy heart.

Duke was right. Kate now belonged with him, as her own plight could endanger Kate's life. If something happened to Kate because of her, she would never forgive herself.

~Chapter 26~

~The Court Date~

It was June tenth, and Savanna had just left the courthouse. The heartache of relinquishing guardianship of Kate was almost unbearable. She avoided eye contact with Duke during the proceedings, and her voice was robotic as she answered questions. She gave her truthful reasons about her life possibly being endangered and agreed to give Duke legal guardianship of Kate. The judge ruled that she stay away from Kate until such a time as the apprehension of her stalker and danger had passed.

Making the situation even worse, was Ashley Oliver, sitting beside Duke with a stoic but smug countenance—her right arm interlocked with his and her massive engagement-ring diamond flashed in the light as her left hand rested on his upper arm.

Savanna was taking long strides to leave the courthouse when her phone rang and Kate's name showed on the caller ID. "Hello Kate!" She did her best to sound upbeat and cheerful. "How's camp," she puffed into the phone as she walked to her car.

"It's–like—the best time so far. There's this boy named Shane who likes me, but Abby thinks he's a little weird. I think he's cute though… and sweet." Kate giggled. "I dropped my cinnamon roll at dinner and ants were all over it, so he gave me his cinnamon roll and I was like… aww. Then, I totally ruined my pink Vans when I stepped in mud yesterday… I'm so flippin' mad. Ugh!" Savanna smiled to hear Kate rattle on with her camp stories. It was like music to her ears. Tears welled in her eyes.

"How are things at home," Kate asked.

Savanna paused as she tried to keep her voice from wavering. "Uh... everything's great… same as usual." Her voice was high pitched as she answered. She didn't intend to break the news to Kate while she was at camp.

"I'm so glad you're enjoying camp. Are you wearing sunscreen outside?"

Kate huffed, "Yes—I'm wearing sunscreen! Worrywart. I gotta go. I love you and miss you, Savanna."

Since this conversation was probably her last with Kate, Savanna's spirit broke as she said, "I love you and miss you too, Kate." She tried to keep her voice steady so that Kate couldn't hear her anguish over the phone.

After she hung up, she leaned on her car, wiped her eyes yet again and placed her aviator gold-framed sunglasses on her face. She turned around to see Duke, in his dark suit and tie, standing near her, and steeled herself for whatever was next.

She moaned to herself. *"What now?"*

He had won. She couldn't imagine what more he had to say to her.

He started speaking before he had even reached her. "Savanna, I—you did the right thing for Kate." He wore a painful expression.

"As was my intention." Her voice was curt. "I hope you don't tell her about this until she returns from camp. There's no reason to ruin her trip."

He opened his mouth to say something, but Savanna continued. "You were right. Kate would be in danger with me, and I would never want to compromise her safety. I hope you keep her in Glenn Oaks. Cash would have wanted her to stay here in the same school for stability reasons—but it's obviously not my decision any longer."

"I'm moving to Glenn Oaks but I have to stay in South Carolina for a couple weeks to close on the selling of my property. I want to make Kate's life as easy as possible since she's already lost her father." He tried to smooth the situation with his words.

"It will delight Kate that you're moving here permanently. I wish you both much happiness." Her words were sincere.

She opened her car door to get in, and he grabbed her forearm. "Savanna—I..."

She brushed his hand aside. "There's nothing more to say. Take care of Kate." Her voice trailed off.

Maintaining composure, she got in her car and was glad to be behind the tinted windows so he could no longer see her face.

As she drove off, she could see him in her rear-view mirror, standing there with his hands at his sides, watching her go. She wept....again. Snuffles and hiccups accompanied her drive home.

~Chapter 27~

A few days after she relinquished guardianship of Kate, the stalker confirmed her decision as wise. The anonymous notes kept coming and someone left them in various places on her property.

The prowler placed a large block of wood, spray painted bright orange, out of view of the cameras with a note tacked to it, and left it in the field at the back of her house. She was sitting on the back porch one evening and noticed it. The note, once more, had mentioned that they would meet up again soon. She couldn't seem to catch whomever was out to get her.

Rachel and Bear asked Logan if he was trying to pursue Savanna, but he denied it and said he was happily remarried to his wife. Her perpetrator left another note on her car while she was grocery shopping and the sheriff had checked on her a few times that week. Cameras in the parking lot gave no answers as the person hid their identity.

After checking the door locks, Savanna walked to each room and checked the windows to make sure they were locked. The camera app on her phone showed the view of her property from the camera and all was clear. She yawned while checking the ammunition in her gun and placed it in the drawer next to her.

She refused to let fear of the stalker take away her freedom to sit outside and watch the sunset. One Friday evening, she made a pitcher of lemonade and carried it out to the back patio after she had finished up the yard work. She showered and put on a light summer sundress. The cicadas and crickets were making their evening debut in a symphony outside, and the day's heat was receding as a slight breeze made its way across the porch. Her weapon of choice was never far from her grasp. Sometimes it was a rifle and sometimes it was her trusty Glock, but this evening, it was a Louisville Slugger.

She leaned her head back on her Adirondack chair, closed her eyes and must have dozed for a bit, because the sun had sank behind the trees and it was almost dark. She stood and stretched. The ice clanked against the pitcher as she opened the patio door to place the glassware inside.

She was startled when she heard footsteps on the side of the house and placed the pitcher back on the table. Her bat was lying across the armrest of the chair. With quiet grace and a firm grip, she grasped the Louisville Slugger and waited out of sight at the edge of the porch. The steps were getting closer, and the cadence slowed. With her arms arced in the air and her heart pounding, she was poised to strike. The intruder had almost rounded the corner to the back porch. A shadow of a man made its appearance. She lunged and swung her aim in that direction. A hand stopped the bat in mid-air, and instinctively, she pounced on her attacker with all her weight. He flung the bat in the opposite direction and shoved her airborne, causing her to land with a thud into a porch chair.

She grabbed the pitcher of lemonade and hurled it toward his head. Even though her aim was on target, he dodged before the glass made contact. The crystal shattered with a dramatic crash as the shards of glass landed in every direction. Lemonade and ice rained down on the porch.

Savanna began looking for her next make-shift weapon, as a deep voice said. "It's just me—Savanna!" Glass crunched beneath his boots as he made his way to her. Her chest was heaving as she tried to catch her breath while her hands gripped the chair.

"What?" She stood. *"Duke?"*

"Don't move!" His voice was gruff. She stood in place on her bare feet, confused at his directive. He bent and hoisted her over his shoulder like a sack of feed.

"What the…?" Her head was facing downward, and she could see the collateral damage left behind on the porch.

He kept her from stepping on the glass shards. His boots crunched through the slivers as he carried her into the house.

He let her down in the kitchen and looked at her. "You ok?"

"I'm fine." She dusted off her cotton dress and rubbed her behind.

"How about you?"

"Never been better. We really have to stop meeting this way," he said as he pulled a couple pieces of glass from his hair. His shirt held splatters of lemonade.

"You know—I do have a doorbell—it's a little safer," she advised.

"I plan to use it next time—you might have a hand-grenade in your arsenal." He smiled down at her.

"Hilarious," she said with dry humor.

"Well—this time, I rang the doorbell, but there was no answer, so I walked around back to see if you might be outside…. turns out… you were." He smiled.

Her lips pulled into a full smile for a second, then her face turned serious. "Right—I guess you are here for Kate's things. I packed them in contain—"

"Savanna, that's not the only reason I'm here," he interrupted.

She stood gaping at him, waiting for the reason.

Duke wasted no time with the preamble. "I was wondering what your honest intentions were with my brother. There didn't seem to be anything ever romantic between the two of you, and I'm sure you could be in a relationship if you wanted. Why would you volunteer to take care of his child for such a long time? I know it couldn't have been just about needing a date to a wedding. You hardly knew Kate, but you took on the role of mother a few weeks after meeting her. I can't seem to find answers as to how this situation came to be." His tone was kind and non-accusing, but his words said otherwise. "It's hard for me to imagine that some woman would take care of someone else's child after only knowing them for a short time. I can't help but think you have an ulterior motive."

She looked down at the floor after what he had said. It was degrading to think he thought so low of her.

Since Duke would leave her life for good today, she didn't want to give him her complete life history and knew she wouldn't change his mind about her only wanting Kate for monetary gain. She gave him the only answer she could. "Duke—I don't know why his path crossed mine in Germany or why we randomly met again in a hardware store years later, but I do know it was fate. It was my destiny to meet Kate and Cash. All I can tell you, is that for once in my life, I belonged to someone—I belonged here in Glenn Oaks—if only for a short while. Kate needed me, and God knows, I needed her." She shrugged, "Maybe someday I'll resolve this problem of a stalker and Kate and I can do lunch and see each other from time to time. If you'll let her."

"Are you going to be ok out here?"

"Oh—yeah, as you are painfully aware, I've got my arsenal of weapons and security cameras." She replied as if to make a joke and waved her hand, "The sheriff still makes rounds out here. I'm fine." She dismissed his concerns and figured he was only being polite by asking. "Thank you for your concern, though. Let me get those containers for you."

The night air smelled of grass and hay as they loaded up Kate's things in the truck. He stopped and turned to her. "I wish you the best and good luck with your stalker situation." Dark, stormy eyes stared into hers as he spoke.

She swallowed and fought to control her composure. "Thanks—and good luck with the wedding and all." She started to walk away.

"Wait, Savanna—just one more thing." He reached into the truck and pulled out a paper bag with handles and handed it to her.

Savanna took the bag and looked inside and her mouth dropped open. "My missing shoe from New Year's Eve. You found it?"

He nodded, "I found it on the ballroom floor as you were leaving with your date. It would be strange for me to keep it, don't you think? I had to return it to where it belongs."

The fact that he'd held onto something that belonged to her all these months was puzzling and now that Kate was leaving her life, he was giving it back to *where it belongs*. She figured that Duke had no deeper meaning behind his statement but she felt those words cut to the bone. It *was* just a shoe after all.

She said goodbye and ran in the house without watching him leave and leaned her back on the door as the bag handle dangled from her fingers. The pain of loss had made its way into her life again.

~Chapter 28~

Guilt, fear and anxiety were Savanna's companions in the days leading up to Kate's return from camp. The feeling of failure washed over her as she had inadvertently abandoned Cash's daughter. Cash's last words echoed in her mind, *"Tell Saint to take care of my girl."*

Her heart hurt to think of how Kate was going to take the news. She hoped Kate would understand that the situation had forced her to let her go for her own safety and well-being. Duke would be the one to tell her when he picked her up.

The anonymous letters continued to show up in different places more frequently, and Savanna had stayed home as much as possible for safety. She was glad Kate had been away at camp and far away from the potential danger. Savanna would stay away from both Kate and Duke as she didn't want to lead danger to them. She didn't know if her predator would harm those she cared about.

She packed a bag in case she needed to leave unexpectedly. Her gun was always within reach and she had taken a few weeks off work. Savanna gave the investigators the letters as evidence, but there were still no leads to the perpetrator. They told her, "we're doing all we can to try to identify who this may be and we won't stop looking."

She was frustrated that law enforcement had made no progress investigating over the last few months. This person knew details of her life, but there were several people who knew her. She had no reason to suspect any of them. Her dating life had been years ago and her ex was behind bars. Cash was gone and Bryan had been his friend. She shook her head in confusion. All she could do was sit and wait…. wait for what, she pondered.

Her anger crushed the fear. The thought of being imprisoned in her own home and taken away from someone she loved, made her blood boil.

She dashed down the hallway and into her bedroom. Savanna flung shoes, summer clothing, jackets and toiletries into a small suitcase. She grabbed the emergency backpack that she previously packed and slung it over her shoulder. With her firearm in tow inside her backpack, she was leaving this temporary prison behind until she could figure out a plan to catch her stalker and get her life back. Adrenaline and determination would carry her to the next phase of her life…. whatever that may be.

Her driveway faded out of view as she sped down the road and onto the major highway. With no other cars in view, she took full advantage of the road with her foot heavy on the accelerator.

The pasture land swept by in a blur as she covered the distance and now and then, she'd check the rear-view mirror just to make sure no one was following her.

She had stopped for gas only once and continued east toward the Atlantic coastline. Her journey was uneventful and the signs for Hilton Head Island were coming into view. This is where she would take respite until she knew the next steps to take.

~Chapter 29~

~Duke~

The memory of Savanna's face haunted his thoughts since the night he collected Kate's belongings. The look in her eyes as they loaded the last of the containers was one of profound emotional pain and loss.

Was the pain in her eyes from the fact that she would no longer have potential to get her hands on Cash's money or genuine sorrow for losing Kate?

She had been very vague when he questioned her about her intentions with his brother and had offered no further insight into her life… insight that he desperately needed. It was as if she was signing off on a chapter, and the details of her past would have been irrelevant. Fate was what she had called it…. her *destiny to meet Cash and Kate—if only for a little while.* She had imprinted those words in his mind.

He was still angry at his brother for going to California and pursuing such a dangerous mission with so much at stake. How could he have left Kate with almost a complete stranger? Duke had always thought they were close growing up. Cash could have asked him to keep Kate during his absence, but he suspected that Cash knew his older brother would talk him out of going after Amy's killers.

How could Savanna not see the potential travesty that would happen by letting Cash go to California? He was furious with her at first, because he needed someone to blame for his brother's death and because she had temporarily taken Kate from him. It was easier to keep her at a distance that way and made ignoring his attraction for her much easier. Ashley, his fiancé, had made no pretense of wanting Savanna gone. She was adamant that Savanna used Kate to slink into the family and get some control and wealth. Had Savanna even known Cash's net worth? Cash had to have known more details about Savanna than he himself did.

He had Kate now and there was no reason for Savanna to keep swirling around in his mind… but she was. He could now close the door on the memory of her ever crossing his path and move on. Kate would eventually be fine.

He had to concentrate on Ashley, the woman he was engaged to. He remembered how they had met at a pub one night. She gave him her business card and told him to call her. It turned out she was a successful attorney. Her family's wealth and status meant they had many social and business connections in South Carolina.

She loved how great they looked together when they were out. She thought her status in society mixed with the heroism of a retired Navy Seal was the perfect combination. They traveled the world together and planned their future.

He asked her to marry him last June since it just seemed like the thing to do. Duke never had deep feelings for her and he couldn't quite place it, but there weren't multiple layers to their relationship.

He knew she had money of her own and wasn't after his. He also knew that he fit into the mold of what she had expected in a husband—a military hero who looked noble to the world, someone who would be beneficial for a potential political career. Superficial love was convenient for him. He wouldn't risk getting hurt like he had in the past.

Ashley also helped to expedite the court proceedings for guardianship of Kate. Her resources enabled them to adjudicate the process for child endangerment. She had all her ducks in a row on this case, almost like she had insight. He felt he was fortunate to have her for that reason.

~Chapter 30~

The rain pelted the windshield as he pulled into Abby's driveway to pick up Kate. He ran a hand through his hair as waves of apprehension hit him. He dreaded the thought of telling Kate that Savanna was no longer her guardian and the reasons why.

"She won't take this well," he thought to himself. She'd already suffered an enormous loss in a short time. He had gotten through hell week training before and he'd get through this the same way. He took a deep breath, got out of the truck and sprinted up to the front door of the house to escape the rain.

Kate bounded to the front door to meet him. "I missed you Uncle Duke!"

He hugged her tight. "I missed you too, Squirt." Duke greeted Abby's family, and they spoke about the trip. The girls were already making plans to go back next year. He and Kate loaded up her things and headed for home.

The rain was still coming down in sheets and the windshield wipers were barely keeping up with their task. "I figured Savanna would ride with you to pick me up."

Duke kept his eyes on the road and didn't reply.

Oblivious to Duke's inner turmoil, she shrugged, "Oh well, that's ok—I'll see her in a few minutes."

Duke pulled off the road and stopped under a bridge because of the torrential rain and lack of visibility. The rain pounding on the cab of the truck came to an abrupt halt as the overpass sheltered them. They could see the deluge in front and back. He figured this would be as good of a time as any to break the news to her. "Kate, there's something I need to tell you."

Her green eyes looked at him with anticipation. "Ok?" Contentment remained on her face. Thunder rolled, and the rain continued to pour.

"Do you remember the anonymous flowers and notes Savanna received for Valentine's Day and then the ones you received from the delivery person at her door?"

She nodded. "Yeah."

He turned to face her, "We believe the person doing that is dangerous, so you would be in danger by staying with Savanna." She stared at him, waiting for him to continue. "The first week you were at camp, Savanna and I had to go to court, and the court awarded me guardianship of you. Savanna gave up her guardianship to protect you from the potential danger of staying with her. We don't know what this stalker person would do to you, or her."

Her mouth opened, but no sound came out.

"It's in your best interest to live with me where you'll be safe."

She shook her head in disbelief. Tears were forming, and she gazed out the windshield at the pouring water rushing off the bridge. Tears morphed into sobs.

"When will I be able to see her," she blubbered.

"Kate—the judge said Savanna can't be near you until the danger has passed. We don't know if or when that will be." He landed the blow he had been dreading the most.

"Do you understand why we had to make this decision?" He asked as he handed her a tissue from the console.

She looked over at him with puffy, tear filled, bright green eyes. "I understand that you are both trying to protect me and look out for me." She sobbed while silence filled the cab.

"But—who's looking out for Savanna," she shouted. Kate wiped her eyes with her hands.

Her question might as well have been a throat punch. As far as he knew, Savanna fought that battle on her own. He imagined the situation scared her. Her hypervigilance and the way she had weapons all over the place meant she knew the danger existed and she would defend herself—alone.

Neither of them spoke. Kate stared out the windshield while the rain poured, and tears streamed down her face. Across from her, Duke sat there running both hands through his hair…. his thoughts developing a strategy.

Kate looked over at him between crying and hiccups. "Help her, Uncle Duke."

~Chapter 31~

The sun warmed her skin, and her favorite scent, which was sunscreen, lulled her into serenity. *Kokomo* by the Beach Boys was playing over the water. The coconut and pineapple frozen drink cooled her down to the perfect temp. The white caps rushed the shore and the rhythm of the waves made her forget her problems for a few more hours. She turned over on her stomach to let the sun bronze her backside. She let her mind go blank and fell asleep listening to the sound of the ocean and sun-tanned vacationers frolicking on the beach. The last few days in a hotel by the water helped her wash away the terror and anxiety. Hunger roused her from her sleep in the sun's warmth.

A Great Dane jumped over her as she lay on her stomach followed by a woman calling for him, "Bentley! Come back here!"

Savanna smiled as the lady tried to keep up with the dog in a long beach cover-up and flip-flops in the sand. The name *Bentley* made her think of the business card Bryan gave her after Cash's death. He disappeared after the funeral. Savanna wondered whatever happened to him. In all the turmoil of the past six months, she hadn't thought about him. Trying to raise Kate, dealing with a stalker and Duke had occupied all her thoughts. She was still amazed at all the details he had known about Amy, Cash and her. Savanna plundered her bag to see if she had brought the card in her wallet, but it wasn't there.

Dressed and showered, she headed down to the café just off the beach and asked for a table for a party of one. The host guided her to a table with two chairs and seated her.

She ordered a meal of chicken with pasta and a glass of Pinot Grigio. Her arms rested on the chair as she leaned back to enjoy the music and breeze.

A man from the bar had glanced in her direction more than once, but she didn't mind. She was sitting alone and figured she undoubtedly appeared to be lonely, sitting there solo. It was almost an invitation. She turned off her phone to avoid the temptation of looking at it and missing out on the beauty of the evening. The stranger at the bar was making his way over to her. "Great," she thought with cynicism.

"Hello — mind if I join you?"

"Yes, I mind," she screamed in her head but her tone remained sweet. "Be my guest." She motioned to the chair across from her and smiled. *"Why not… what have I got to lose?"* Her creep-o-meter was at a ten, but she squashed her judgment of the bald man before her. Danger wasn't in the forefront of her mind since they were in a public place, and she was away from Glenn Oaks. She decided to be kind to this lonely stranger.

"Mason McCann." He extended his hand.

"Kelsey Donovan," she replied as she shook his hand. Savanna congratulated herself for her new, cool alias, at a second's notice. *"Not bad."*

"You looked so lovely sitting there—I couldn't help but come over and introduce myself."

"It's a pleasure to meet you." Graciousness coursed through her words.

"Believe me, the pleasure is all mine." He matched her politeness.

"Gag." Savanna laughed to herself. *"Let this evening end sooner than later."*

A smile breached the corner of her mouth, but it was because of the humor playing in her mind.

The only hair on his entire head was his thick, salt and pepper gray beard and mustache. Large, square-framed glasses rested on his nose and magnified his eyes in an unflattering manner. She thought at any moment he'd tell her to give him his red stapler, like Milton on Office Space.

His voice was nasal and whiny, and his teeth protruded as he talked.

The server asked if he would like his meal served at her table. He looked at Savanna for permission.

"Oh—uh—sure."

They conversed about his many travels and his tragic divorce from a wife who 'just up and left him for another man.' He talked about his love of boats and how he had rented a twenty-eight foot cabin cruiser while he was staying there.

He asked Kelsey her story.

"I live in Tampa, Florida and I'll be meeting friends here in a couple days. I have a boyfriend named Max who unfortunately had to work during our trip." She smiled at him.

He stared at her with his chin resting in his hand, enthralled in her story.

At the end of the meal, Mason paid. At first, she protested, since she figured he would expect something more from her in return—but he insisted on paying.

"Thank you for the company and the meal, Mason."

"And thank you—Kelsey." He paused as if he couldn't remember her name for a second.

She excused herself and headed for her room. Her feet moved swiftly down the lantern- lit path, to the lobby, to brush him from her proximity as soon as possible.

Savanna mulled over her day as she brushed her teeth and completed her skin care routine. She closed the blinds and put on a matching T-shirt and short set. Relaxation of her day and exhaustion of the evening meal took hold of her, and sleep consumed her. Tomorrow she'd decide what her plans were… tonight she'd power sleep.

~Chapter 32~

She slapped at the bedside table without aim to shut off the alarm-clock, but it kept blaring and jostled her from sleep. The noise wasn't the alarm-clock. The red light in her room was blinking a red glow across the wall, choreographed with the annoying fire alarm.

"Oh, for the love of...." She shoved her feet into flip-flops, put on a bra, then threw her phone into her backpack along with her purse. The fire alarm was assaulting her ear drums. Her flip-flops slapped the bottom of her feet in a clipped cadence as she headed for the exit along with other guests.

Hotel guests lined the perimeters of the building outside and Savanna made her way to the back of the crowd. She spotted Mason McCann in the crowd staring at her without expression. She looked toward the building and then back to where he was standing, but he had disappeared into the crowd of on-lookers.

Two fire-trucks pulled to the front entrance. Firefighters entered the building. No flames or smoke appeared, and the guests were murmuring their theories on what had happened.

As she reached up to swat at an insect flying around her head, she saw the crowd move toward the building as the firefighters gave an "all clear." Savanna took a step forward to move with the crowd.

~Chapter 33~

As she trudged along, a large hand stopped her progress and clamped across her mouth. "Don't scream—walk with me—Kelsey. I am armed and I will kill you, or anyone who gets in my way," the voice behind her whispered, inches from her ear.

In the darkness, he guided her away from the building and out of earshot of guests. The path was dark except for a few lamps in the distance. He goaded her forward in silence toward a boat dock, lined with cabin cruisers. The boats bobbed on the water as the waves lapped them. "You won't be needing this." He yanked her backpack from her shoulder and tossed it into the tall grass where the pier met the shore.

Terror gripped her as he said her alias and discarded her backpack which held her phone. There would be no way to summon help and no one could find her. "Why are you doing this?"

He grabbed her wrist and twisted her arm behind her as he turned her to look at his face. She gasped at the sight of the man standing before her. The bald head now had a full head of slicked back, wavy, dark hair. He had removed the facial hair and large framed, thick glasses.

His eyes held manic rage, and alcohol tainted his breath. His grip was punishing, as though he hated her existence. "I'm not Mason McCann and you're not Kelsey Donovan from Tampa, Florida. You have no boyfriend named Max. You are Savanna St. James from Glenn Oaks, Georgia. A cute little magpie told me where I might find you." He regurgitated the words of the notes he had given to her.

"My Dearest Savanna," he mocked. "I told you we would meet again this summer. You belong to me. I hope you enjoyed the Ranunculus… pink ones—your favorite."

He tried to plant his mouth on hers but she twisted her face to the side and avoided the repulsive contact. "I don't belong to anyone—least of all you. I wouldn't have you if you stripped naked and dipped yourself in 24-karat gold." The words were forceful.

Her ear rang and she saw stars when his hand struck the left side of her head. If he hadn't had a grip on her, she would have fallen backward. She knew she had to regain her equilibrium and fight. Her knee came up to assault his crotch, but missed. The attempt only fueled his anger and his palm struck the left side of her mouth. She could feel blood and sweat trickling down the left side of her face and into her eye. The mixed taste of metal and salt was on her tongue from the blow to her bottom lip.

"I see you're a fighter and should learn to control that mouth. I plan to teach you a lesson though." She tried to run from his grasp but he grabbed her arm and twisted it behind her. She protested in pain as he shoved her forward.

When I'm done with you, I'm going to find the little brat who lived with you—Kate I believe, and when I'm done with her, I'm going to find her uncle."

"You stay away from them! It's me you're after. They've done nothing to you. I'll do anything you ask—just leave them alone."

"We're going on a little romantic midnight cruise—move." He continued to shove her toward the end of the dock to board a twenty-eight foot cabin cruiser.

She guessed this was the rented boat Mason McCann had mentioned at dinner. How had she been in such oblivion as she had sat there and ate with him? She lamented at her own foolishness.

Savanna's shoulder ached from the angle he held her arm. As her captor walked and shoved, he finally pushed her onto the boat. Her head was throbbing, and sweat was making her T-shirt stick to her body. The boat rocking made balancing more difficult. Her eye had swollen more and impeded her vision. Before she realized, he was placing a zip tie to her wrists in her lap.

"You're worthless. No wonder you're still alone. It seems so pitiful, don't you think?" He held a knife close to her throat. "I don't know what I ever saw in you," he said, and laughed at her.

She smelled the stench of alcohol on his breath, and tried to move away from the knife he was holding close to her throat.

The boat gave a warning screech as he started the ignition. Her legs stuck to the white vinyl as the boat moved along the water to the opening of the channel. The moon was full and made a sparkling beam along the water's surface. The wind on her face dried the blood and sweat to her skin. She could feel the swelling increase in her eye. After they had traveled a few miles out to sea, he cut the engine and stepped down three steps to the cabin below. It was dark and Savanna could see nothing except the glints of light from the moon on the water. A light shone down below in the cabin. The boat swayed back and forth on the water. Dizziness crested and receded just like the waves. Strength was leaving her.

Moments later, he resurfaced to the deck, pulled her up from the cushion and cupped her chin in his hand. "See, we get to spend some quality time together, out here on the ocean… just you and me….my dearest Savanna. Did you think I would buy you all your favorite flowers and then not come for you?" His breath reeked of whiskey, and in one hand, still held a knife. His mouth tried to claim hers again, but this time her aim was better. Thanks to adrenaline, she landed a hard blow to his man parts and dropped him like a sack of rocks to the deck.

His head bumped the side of the boat as he fell and his mouth gushed threats and profanities at her as he held his groin and head, writhing in pain. He rolled on to his side in the fetal position. "Oh… son of a…" The knife had dropped from his clutches.

The swelling hindered her vision, but she could grasp the knife from the deck. She needed to cut the plastic around her wrists but couldn't in the darkness. Her tied wrists were of little use.

The zip tie binding her wrists was cutting into her flesh. She remembered watching a video once about how to escape them, but her brain couldn't recall. *"Think, Savanna."*

After a few moments, she took the end of the plastic cord between her teeth and pulled the plastic band even tighter. Her shoulder protested in pain as she raised her hands above her head, and then dropped them down and apart. Savanna shrieked from the pain. Nothing happened except for shearing pain where the tie bound her. She garnered her strength, and tried again, as her kidnapper's groans continued from the floor of the deck. The plastic pieces broke apart and her heart leaped with a small victory.

Her mind was racing with ideas for survival. The gun—she needed to find the gun. Her face was throbbing and her legs wanted to fold beneath her, but she kept her focus on the task. Savanna took a step down into the cabin and fell the rest of the two steps below deck.

She pulled herself upright and braced herself at the edge of a foldout bed. The dried blood had pasted her hair to her face. The swelling completely impeded her vision in one eye.

A shelf rested above the pullout bed, and on top, rested his firearm. She could see the tip of the gun. She steadied herself along the wall of the boat and willed her body to scoot along the bed until she reached the shelf. Her shoulder was stiff and painful with movement, so she used her other hand to boost her arm up to grab the gun. Fingers connected with the metal. Her soul rejoiced with a hint of hope of survival. She knew that time was her enemy and it wouldn't be long until he had recovered from her assault on him. She checked to see that there was ammo, and the magazine was in place. Her hands shook as she worked. She could hear him stirring on the deck above, and knew her time for a chance at survival, was running out.

She held the gun in one hand and stumbled toward the door. As she emerged from the cabin, she could see his silhouette as he pushed himself up from the deck floor and onto the cushions. He was still slurring profanities at her.

She grasped the gun in both her hands as she took aim at him. A half-empty bottle of Jack Daniels rolled around on deck as the waves gently tossed the boat. She watched him grab the bottle and take a long slug of it. He leaned back on the cushions and exhaled.

A glimpse of her shown in the moonlight, along with the gun she had cradled in her hands. "You won't do it—you won't kill me. You'll die out here on the Atlantic, just like I've planned." He gave an intoxicated laugh. "You're as good as shark bait, Savanna."

She stayed still and silent. The pitch of the boat threatened to knock her out of her stance. She planted her feet, poised to kill him if he tried anything.

"Take me back to the dock," she demanded in a hoarse voice.

He didn't obey her, but just watched her stand there.

"I mean it—I'll kill you." Her voice shook. He took another swig of booze and like a cheetah, lunged at her.

She fired the gun but missed her target because of the rocking of the boat. He knocked the weapon from her hands and tackled her to the floor. The gun slid across the deck and back toward her.

She felt his hands around her throat. Her air was being obstructed by the pressure of his fingers as his body lay half covering hers. As the pressure of his hands around her neck increased, she felt a pop in her throat and gasped for air.

The gun slid close to her hand, and she grasped it with every fiber of her being. She pointed the gun point-blank to his side and squeezed the trigger. The sound of gunfire splintered her eardrums. He groaned, and limpness took over his body. His hands loosened their grip on her throat, and she felt warm liquid oozing on her.

Savanna took a large gulp of air as his grip slackened. Her chest was heaving as she tried to recover air into her lungs. She only had the strength to partially roll his heavy body off her. Pain was surging through her throat, her shoulder and her head were throbbing. A cracked lip and parched throat added to her misery. Faintness set in as she let the world around her swallow her up in dreams.

~Chapter 34~

Duke pulled into his drive-way with Kate, thankful to have her back home from camp. She sat in silence the rest of the way home after they had discussed his newly gained guardianship of her. She still sniffled and her eyes were still red from crying.

He needed to see Savanna, but didn't want to take Kate with him for safety reasons. He remembered Momma Lynn telling him to call if he needed anything. Well today, he needed her.

He dialed Momma Lynn's Café and one of her employees answered. He drummed his fingers on his desk waiting for her to pick up the phone. "This is Momma Lynn, how may I help?"

"Uh—Momma Lynn, this is Duke Hollingsworth and I have a big favor to ask."

"Well, Duke Honey, what is it?" Her maternal voice took over.

"I think Savanna might be in serious trouble and might need my help—I wondered if you might look after Kate for a few hours until my fiancé, Ashley, gets in town."

"Happy to darlin, just give me 'bout twenty minutes to finish this shift and I'll be right out to your place. Imma bring y'all somethin' to eat. Is that alright?"

He smiled at her kindness. "You bet, Momma Lynn, if it's no trouble—thank you."

He drove up to Savanna's place, and no lights were on except for the outside lamps. The blinds were closed. His boots clunked on the porch as he made his way to the front door. His knuckles gave a hard rap, and he rang the doorbell several times.

No answer.

An uneasiness haunted him. He walked around to the back of the house calling out her name to avoid scaring her. The porch was empty. He climbed the steps of the back porch and beat on the door. "Savanna. It's Duke!"

Silence.

Thoughts of her harmed inside the house, permeated his mind. He grabbed a bright orange, spray- painted block of wood from the back lawn, and with force, broke the storm door glass window. The glass door opened as he unfastened it. His boot hit the back door with a thud. The door frame splintered as the door burst open. "Savanna… it's Duke. Are you in here? Savanna?"

Duke searched every corner of the house, but there was no trace of her. The alarm hadn't sounded with his entry. He figured she must have left in a hurry, and hadn't set the alarm. Her car was also missing from the garage.

He stood in her office looking around. His eyes fastened on a large manila envelope with the name CASH HOLLINGSWORTH on the front. It sat at the corner of her desk. Duke pulled the papers out, and along with them, fell a business card.

BRYAN BENTLEY –Private Investigator

The back of the card read:

Savanna,

Call me if you need anything or have questions about Cash's arrangements—Truly sorry for your loss. He was like a brother to me.--Bryan

Duke looked up from the card and figured that Bryan could tell him something about Savanna.... anything. Maybe Cash told Bryan details about Savanna. He had spoken with him at Cash's funeral and Bryan had offered his condolences on the loss of his brother and sister-in-law.

He dialed the number on the card and prayed Bryan would answer.

"Bentley," said the curt male voice on the other end.

"Bryan—this is Duke Hollingsworth, Cash's older brother......."

There was a pause, "Duke, what can I do for you, man?"

"I need some Intel. Someone has been following Savanna since February this year. They leave notes around her property. She was forced to give up custody of Kate since the situation caused child endangerment. I can't find her—I wasn't too concerned with her well-being since Cash gave her guardianship of Kate—I was angry with her. When Kate found out about it, she was terrified for Savanna. Can you help me out?"

"Duke—Cash told me how he met Savanna. She had no clue about the extent of his wealth. He felt her love for Kate was genuine."

Bryan told Duke about her brief previous marriage to a pilot named Creed Kelley who had gone to prison for cocaine dealings and the abuse she had endured at his hands. "Cash had told me that it was fate that he met Savanna, because it gave him the chance to avenge his wife's death. He had asked me to do a background check on Savanna before he'd gone to California. Her background check came back snow white except that Creed filed a police report stating she had stabbed him in the leg but didn't file charges against her."

A storm of emotions overwhelmed Duke at the information given to him. So—his brother *had* done research on Savanna before leaving Kate with her. His anger surfaced at the thought that someone had mistreated her. He had to find out exactly who was after her and help her before it was too late. He had already lost his brother. *"I don't plan on losing Savanna. What a fool I've been."* He ran a hand over his face.

"I'll do everything I can to help you find Savanna," Bryan said. "Cell phone and credit card usage would give me a lot of information on her whereabouts. I'll get back with you after I do some research."

"I appreciate it," Duke said.

~Chapter 35~

Ashley's Mercedes sat in his driveway as he pulled in. He walked in the door with worry-lines on his face and she greeted him with a kiss. "You look like you've lost your best friend."

"It's Savanna—she's not home." Duke's voice held concern.

Ashley raised her brows. "And?"

"Uncle Duke, how is she?" Kate interrupted with a troubled expression.

"I'm not sure. I couldn't find her, but I'm having an old friend of your Dad's investigate where she might have gone."

"Bryan—the guy from California who told us about my dad dying?"

Duke nodded.

Ashley poured herself a glass of wine and leaned on the counter. "She's probably gone back to her ex-husband

Chris Kelley or Clark… I don't remember…. something Kelley." She said with disinterest and Duke stared at her.

"How did *you* know about her ex-husband?" His eyes narrowed.

Ashley finished her sip of wine and shrugged. "I had some connections of mine investigate her for any dirt to help you gain guardianship of Kate. I figured anything we could uncover would help us. I found out she divorced a pilot, and I spoke to him myself, to find out more — anything to help our cause. I like to win." She inspected her nails after she spoke.

Duke crossed his arms in front of him. "You spoke with Creed Kelley?" He glared at her and waited for a response.

"Yes—at length. He said Savanna just left him for no reason after a few months of marriage. I wanted to know if she had any drug or alcohol related issues or a sordid past. He said she had accused him of abuse and that she had made up the allegations to get out of the marriage to be with another man." She took another sip of wine. "He was doing time for drug crimes involving transporting cocaine."

"Did you tell Creed anything about Savanna? Did you mention that she was guardian over Kate?"

"Why the sudden hostility? I might have mentioned that she had something we wanted. He seemed to be more willing to give information after I told him a few things about her."

"When did you contact him?" His tone was icy.

"Uh… I don't know—maybe in mid-January." Her tone was aloof as she gave another shrug.

His heart kicked his chest hard. With that revelation, Duke guessed that the Valentine's Day flowers could have been from Creed. "And you didn't think to tell me this information considering Kate lived with her at the time?" His face reddened.

Ashley walked over to him and placed a hand on his arm in a patronizing gesture. "I was trying to help you get Kate, sweetheart. We both know Savanna was only after Cash's money."

His gaze leveled with hers as he turned to face her. "Do we?" His volume increased. He pulled away from her touch as he pulled his phone from his pocket. "You do not understand the danger you've put her in." Ashley rolled her eyes at his statement. "Not to mention, you could have gotten Kate killed too," he bit out.

Duke's phone lit up. "Bryan, what's up?"

"Creed Kelley—her ex—I just found out—the FAA revoked his pilot license, and he's got a rap sheet for multiple domestic abuse charges on different women. He's got a history of using an aircraft for drug smuggling. He even attempted murder on the last woman he was with. This guy's got some issues. He looks like a fine upstanding citizen in his pictures but he's a snake. He's doing time, but is up for parole in a month.

Duke ran a hand through his hair and paced. "None of this makes sense."

"Let me call you back with more info, brother," Bryan said, and the phone went silent on the other end.

"She's out of your life now. You have Kate. She's not your problem anymore." Ashley interjected after his phone call ended.

"I love her… he has to get her back," Kate said as she stood with her arms crossed while looking at Ashley.

"Are you in love with her too, Duke," Ashley accused. Her face held disbelief at his possible feelings for Savanna.

No answer came from his lips. His arms rested at his sides as Ashley continued. "After all the effort I've put into this relationship—not to mention all the strings I pulled to get Kate for you. I should have seen this coming." Ashley shook her head. "She used Kate to get closer to you. Either Hollingsworth brother would have sufficed for her.... as long as she gained your wealth. She even pretended to care for a thirteen-year-old, to get close to you. You are blind Duke Hollingsworth if you don't see it. What a fool! Clearly you aren't thinking with your brain."

Kate gasped at Ashley's tirade and the implication that Savanna was only using her. She covered her mouth as Ashley raged, and then said, "*What?* You think Savanna only pretended to love me and wanted to be my mother to get to Duke?" Ashley ignored the question as though Kate was irrelevant.

Kate and Duke stood watching Ashley's speech turn into a fit of anger. She slid her shoes on as she talked and threw her engagement ring across the room where it hit the wall with a ping. "We—are—done!" The door slammed on her way out.

Neither of them looked out the window to watch her leave. Duke hugged Kate. "That can't be true about Savanna because I've always felt wanted and loved when I'm around her," Kate said.

"Ashley doesn't know what she's talking about. She's not a good person," Duke said and Kate nodded as she hugged him.

Their attention turned back to the plan to help Savanna and Duke pulled away. "Kate, I may need to leave when I find out her whereabouts, is it ok if I call Rachel and Bear to see if they can keep you until I get back?"

"Yeah, it's fine with me—just—I want her back Uncle Duke." Kate wiped a tear from her eye with fear that Savanna may never make it back to her

Duke made a call to Bear Covington and explained their plight. He arranged for Kate to stay with them. When Rachel found out about the ominous situation, she was beside herself with worry and was happy to help watch Kate.

"Duke, we'd asked Logan, her date for New Year's Eve, if he knew anything about these notes Savanna was getting, but he's back with his ex-wife. I'll keep trying to call Savanna. I feel like a fool…Savanna acted like it was no-big-deal about the anonymous flowers and note. I thought all of this was behind her. Oh—I've been so caught up in my own life that I didn't realize Savanna was in such danger. I just thought she had a secret admirer… not a stalker." She sighed. "She never asks for help and is such a recluse that I didn't want to impose on her."

"It's not your fault Rachel, trust me. I've treated her so much worse."

Duke prepared an overnight bag and was ready to go the moment he heard from Bryan. His gut held uneasiness. There was something else amiss, but he couldn't quite place it.

An hour later, the phone rang and Bryan told him, "The last ping on Savanna's phone is near a resort on Hilton Head Island." With that information, Duke threw his belongings in the truck and headed out to find Savanna.

~Chapter 36~

The distance to Hilton Head Island seemed to drag on forever. He knew Savanna was in grave danger. He could feel it. Duke hoped and prayed he wasn't too late. Her face came to his mind—the elation and joy that he witnessed while she was riding the horse that day. He hadn't seen her countenance as bright as that since he'd met her. He could still see her blonde hair blowing behind her as she sat in the saddle and he recounted the self-control he had to exercise when they got back to the barn. He wanted to hold her close after he helped her down off his horse, but he forced his hands off her waist. He shook off those feelings and reminded himself that he was an engaged man as she looked at him with those blue-green eyes.

His denial of feelings for her should have been the first clue that Ashley was not "the one" for him. How could he have been so deceived regarding his ex-fiancé? He told himself that Savanna was just after Cash's money to deter any feelings toward her. It hadn't helped that Ashley had been campaigning that same idea to keep him on track.

"I'm so sorry, Savanna," he muttered under his breath. He tried calling her phone again but it went straight to voice-mail.

Bryan agreed to meet him in Hilton Head to help him find her. He understood why Cash would have had Bryan as a friend, and as a bonus, Bryan Bentley also had connections in law enforcement in South Carolina, which would benefit Duke's mission to find and rescue Savanna.

As Duke arrived in Hilton Head, Bryan called him to say he discovered that she had used a credit card for a hotel a few days ago. "Meet me at the resort," Bryan told him.

"This guy is good," he thought.

Duke was on a mission as he entered the hotel lobby, the bellhop stepped out of his way to avoid a collision. As the hotel clerk was finishing a transaction with the customer in front of him, he ran a hand through his hair and exhaled to stay calm.

When the patrons were out of his way, he pulled out his phone and showed the clerk a picture of Savanna. "Hi— I'm Duke Hollingsworth and I need to find Savanna St. James. She checked into this hotel a few days ago and I believe she may be in danger. Can you tell me what room she's—" Duke didn't get to finish his question.

"Sir, I can't tell you which room the guests are in, it's against our policy." The girl at the desk apologized as her gold plated name tag gleamed with the name, AMY engraved.

"Could I speak with your supervisor—please, Amy? Someone is in danger here and time is of the essence." He was ready to punch someone. The thought of Savanna being in harm's way had driven him to desperation. He was ready to walk around to the computer and look it up himself but that might land him in jail. "Come on," he willed them to hurry under his breath.

A man in a uniform greeted him. "Sir, what can I do for you?"

"Are you the one in charge here?"

"Yes, sir."

"I need to find out if Savanna St. James is in her room. I believe this man could possibly endanger her." He held up a picture of Creed Kelley.

"Sir, I can call her room for you, but it's against policy to tell you what room she's stay—"

Duke interrupted. "Yes—call her room, please." The man in charge dialed her room several times as they waited.

"I'm afraid there's no answer, sir." The man said apologetically.

"Could you have someone go to the room and see if they can get in? This could be a matter of life and death."

The man looked at him and made a call. "Sir if you'll wait right here, I'll have someone check."

"Ok—fine… thanks." The lack of urgency annoyed Duke, but he controlled his temper and his temptation to lay into the man at the counter.

He dialed Bryan Bentley but his phone went to voice-mail. Pacing back and forth in the hotel lobby, he waited to hear if she was in her room.

The manager motioned for him to come to the desk. As Duke walked toward him, the man shook his head and said that the room still had her belongings but she was not there, nor had she checked out. "Thanks," Duke said as his mind started conjuring a plan.

Duke stopped pacing as he caught sight of the name tag again. AMY, it said. Like lightning striking his brain, thoughts of the conversation he had with Bryan at Cash's funeral came to mind. *"Amy and I were very close. I wanted to find her killers as badly as Cash. Too bad Cash died trying. My condolences are with you and Kate,"* Bryan had said. Cash's stomach lurched as suspicions of Bryan related to Amy's death hit him. Anger and confusion set in as he tried to construct reasons for Cash's death and Savanna's disappearance. Bryan was the common denominator who seemed to know everything about both of them. *"How could I not see that?*

At the back of the hotel, was a view of the Atlantic and a peer in the distance with boats docked. He moved toward the peer in search of any clue until Bryan arrived. An ocean breeze blew his hair as he walked, and a pack of seagulls squawked in the distance as he headed in the water's direction. The smell of the saltwater did little to assuage his nerves.

He walked along the path until he came to a clearing where the peer met the shore. Boats were empty and dotted the peer. He prayed that he would find something—anything that would lead him to her. He planted his foot at the shore where the peer started and stood there trying to imagine scenarios for her abduction.

He turned and a tan backpack with turquoise letters caught his eye. The letters were SKS identical to the one Kate had bought Savanna for Christmas. The man carrying the backpack had slung it across his shoulder as if he had just picked it up from the grass. Duke ran toward him and caught up with him from behind. "Excuse me! Hey—with the backpack!" The man with the matted hair kept walking and Duke walked alongside him. "I'm afraid you have my backpack." The man glanced sideways at him, "Beat it. Backpack's mine. I found it."

Duke pulled the backpack, and the man held on.

"Look, it's mine but I'll give you one-hundred dollars cash for it."

"Get lost, it's mine, dude." The man picked up the pace and ran.

Duke got in his face and shoved him into the side of a stack of beach lounge chairs while holding the man's throat in his right hand. "I'm going to give you a choice. You can take the money and hand over the backpack or I'll rearrange your face and take the backpack. A choice you'd better make quickly." He said it with steel in his voice.

The man held out his hand for the money and Duke gave it to him while grabbing the backpack from the man's shoulder, but not before giving one last shove.

A cell phone and a brown leather purse were inside. Women's purses were no-man's-land to him, but this time, wild horses couldn't have prevented him from opening that bag. Hope sprang forth as he opened the wallet to see Savanna's Georgia driver's license. He looked around trying to imagine which direction her kidnapper had taken her.

His instincts directed his eyes toward the water and the boats at the dock. She had to be out there somewhere….

he could feel it. "Hold on Savanna, I'm coming for you," he uttered while scanning the water. Duke walked back up to the hotel parking lot, in search of her car, and as he suspected, it was still there.

Bryan called to say his ETA was about an hour away and that he had some South Carolina law enforcement on the way. An hour was going to seem like a painful eternity.

A seagull squawked in the distance and Duke caught a glimpse of Bryan walking toward him.

"Sorry it took so long. Find out anythin—" Bryan tried to ask as he walked toward Duke, but before he could finish, Duke turned around and lunged at him. Anger lit his eyes. He had a vice grip on Bryan's throat as he backed him into the nearest wall. The rage he felt for the loss of his brother, sister-in-law and Savanna had crested.

"What have you done with Savanna?"

Bryan wheezed while trying to take in air as Duke's hand crushed his airway. Duke decreased the pressure to allow Bryan to speak.

Bryan coughed, "What the hell are you talking about," he gasped.

Bryan felt the cold metal at his temple as Duke held a gun to his head. "You'd better tell me everything you know," he gritted out.

Bryan didn't move but his eyes cut sideways to see the gun pointed at his head.

Silence.

Duke tightened his grip on Bryan's throat once again as Bryan tried to fight him off.

"Okay," Bryan choked out. "Amy and I had an affair when Cash was overseas. It was brief and I felt such guilt about it. Then Amy died, and I wanted to help Cash anyway I could. That's why I devoted myself to finding her killers while Cash moved to Georgia to raise his daughter."

He coughed once again. "Cash didn't leave Kate with you because you were going through your own personal hell and he thought raising his daughter might be too much for you. That's why he made the will before leaving and awarded guardianship to Savanna." He sucked air into his lungs. "I'll never forgive myself for what I did to Cash, but I have tried my best to rectify it. He never knew about Amy and me."

Duke released his hold on Bryan and dropped the gun to his side. He ran a hand through his hair then punched Bryan in the mouth with a right hook. "That's for my brother."

Bryan didn't fight back, but said, "I guess I deserved that," as he felt his mouth.

"I swear man, I'm not involved in Savanna's disappearance. I'm trying my best to help find her. We're wasting time here," Bryan said as he wiped the blood from his mouth with the back of his hand. "Whether you believe me or not, Cash was like a brother to me. I just got too close to Amy when she was lonely and I deeply regret it. The only way to show my remorse is to help bring Savanna back to Kate….and you. I'll die trying anyway." He held up his right forearm which bore the same tattoo as Cash. "Death before dishonor," he said as Duke looked at the words on Bryan's forearm.

    Duke nodded and holstered his gun under his shirt as a silent truce.

~Chapter 37~

As the horizon swallowed the sun, Bryan and Duke spent the last few hours organizing a search party. After a few phone calls and skilled detective work, Bryan confirmed they identified a cabin cruiser Creed Kelley had rented. The coast guard was helping in the search. A few hours passed with no sight of the boat on the water. The darkness was going to hamper their efforts. Their theory was that the boat had drifted further out to sea. Making matters worse, no radio contact reached the vessel.

Duke tried not to think about what might happen if a ship failed to see them on the water. He prayed once again for her safety and pushed back the pang of defeat that kept trying to capture his thoughts. He wouldn't allow it. She was going to survive. He had to continue to believe that. "Hang in there, Savanna. I'm coming to rescue you," he said once again.

~Chapter 38~

In her dreams, Savanna could see Creed handing her pink flowers on Valentine's Day and dropping to one knee. "Will you marry me?" Happiness coursed through her. He had been a gentleman and opened doors for her, brought her coffee, watched movies with her and showed her off to his friends. Then, she saw him standing at the altar waiting for her to walk down the aisle toward him. She was walking alone. No one gave her away when she reached him at the altar. She could see their guests—a few military friends along with a few of his family members. Gratefulness filled her as she reached him. She was thankful for this man who came into her life and filled the loneliness. He was standing there looking so handsome… how lucky she was.

Her dream took her to Brodie who was sitting beside her as she rubbed his head and spoke to him in her usual baby talk. "Sweet widdle Bwodie," she said. His blonde fur was soft. She hugged him.

Visions of Creed's enraged face now invaded her dreams. He was slamming her against the wall after she had questioned him about his infidelity. He was shouting at her about how crazy and paranoid she was to think he was cheating on her. His hand came across her face. He was shaking her. She fought. The dream pulled her in further. He bashed her face into the wall. Savanna pushed back. She waited until another woman came into view—a woman who was kissing Creed in front of her—now is my chance to leave.... I can escape this marriage. Someone else will distract him and take my place. I should warn her. I have to escape. Divorce papers drifted through her visions....her decree of freedom from this tyrant. "Run—I have to get away."

Her home in Georgia wafted through her dream. The feel of freedom and warmth of home greeted her along with the green pastures surrounding her house. A pink and orange sunset surrounded a lush green field. She could see Mr. Perkins helping her put fence posts in the ground.

Momma Lynn was bringing her a piece of pie.

Rachel hugged her and handed her a glass of champagne.

Visions of Kate's sweet face drifted into view. She could see ants on a cinnamon bun and someone handing Kate another clean one. Kate's laugh filled her mind as she drifted through her dream. She's twirling around in a dress that she's wearing to a school dance. Kate's cheering before a football crowd and smiling… so happy. Love fills her heart as Kate hugs her.

Cash is holding out his hand for her to take it. Savanna feels the warmth of his hand. She walks with him and tells him, "Cash, you shouldn't have gone to California and Kate misses you desperately. I miss you, Duke misses you. We needed you here with us. We met up in Georgia just like you said we would when we were in Germany. You were the only one missing. We buried you under a beautiful Magnolia tree. I'm sorry I couldn't keep Kate for you. I wanted to keep her safe. Forgive me for failing you."

Cash looked at her. "It's ok Savanna you'll be with her. You still have her" he said in her dream.

"No! You don't understand, she's with Duke and Ashley now. I couldn't protect her from danger. I'm coming with you Cash. Don't let go of my hand."

She could see a bright light, it was beautiful. Cash released her hand. "You can't come with me. You have to stay. Kate needs you," he said.

She cried. "Cash, don't let go of my hand. I don't have Kate anymore. I don't belong with them!" Cash looked at her with a kind angelic smile. "Go back Savanna. It's not time to give up yet. You belong with them." He was shaking his head.

Duke's face drifted into her dream. She was looking down at him from her saddle. He was leading the horse by the reins. Her heart was about to burst with love for him at that moment. She could feel her hair blowing in the breeze. She could feel him lift her down from the horse. He was standing in front of her with his hands on her waist. His dark blue eyes were looking into hers.

She was dancing with him in a ballroom and he was holding her. Etta James was singing her song: At Last—my love has come along—my lonely days are over. She could feel them floating around on the dance floor. His hand was on her back and her hand was in his. His dark blue eyes were looking into hers again.

Duke's deep voice, and random words, "Hold on Savanna, I'm coming to rescue you," invaded her dream.

~The Search~

The search went on through the night. Thanks to Bryan, Duke could join a search and rescue team and keep looking for Savanna. The sun was making its debut on the horizon as another day began.

There had been a few small tropical showers but still their search efforts forged ahead. The morning dampened his spirits as nothing but blue sea stretched out before them with no sign of a boat. Fatigue plagued him and he took a swig of coffee from his thermos.

A radio call interrupted his thoughts. "Cabin cruiser type of boat — [Static] — visual… two passengers on board"… [Static].

Hope lurched in his soul. "God, please let it be her." He looked heavenward as he said a prayer. "Please let her be alive."

The crew of the boat and the helicopter headed to the coordinates where the boat was seen. As they scanned the Atlantic, a small vessel came into view, getting larger as they neared it. The glint of silver on the bow of the boat sparkled in the sun.

The helicopter lowered closer to the sea. The sound of the chopper blades accompanied the rescue as they lowered the crew member down to the boat. The water swirled below with the wind from the helicopter. As his vessel neared the area, he could see two people lying on the deck. One was laying across the other. He willed his mind to focus only on the task at hand. "Don't think—just get her on board that helicopter." He coached himself as he boarded the cabin cruiser.

~The Rescue~

Upon arrival to the boat, Duke made a quick visual sweep of the area and saw Creed Kelley partially lying across Savanna with what appeared to be a gunshot to his torso. His body showed mottling and cyanosis. The gun near him was evidence that Savanna had defended herself. His blood drenched her side.

Duke and a crew-member rolled Creed's body off Savanna. The injuries had swollen her face and Duke barely recognized her. Blood plastered her hair to her face. He checked for signs of life and to his relief, she was still breathing. Bruises marked her throat.

He wanted to reassure her if she could hear him, and he bent down to her ear. "Savanna, you're going to be ok. I'm here now. We're getting you help."

He helped to lift her limp body into the rescue basket and secured her. The basket dangled in the air as it ascended to meet the helicopter. He watched until they pulled Savanna into the aircraft.

Duke noticed an Atlantic Police Marine Patrol Unit boat on the scene. All he cared about was meeting Savanna at the hospital as he boarded a boat taking him back to shore.

~Savanna~

The sound of helicopter blades slicing through the air in the distance, drifted in and out of her consciousness. Her body was being swayed back and forth, back and forth. Birds were screeching above her. The pain—her head and face—throat.

"Savanna." A deep voice called her name. She couldn't answer. She wanted to answer, but no sound escaped her throat. She willed her eyes to open, but they refused. Her limbs wanted to move, but tons of gravity held them captive. "It's ok, Savanna." A hand stroked her head. Her body was being lifted. Where is she going? Is this a dream? She needed help. She should try to scream for help. No sounds came from her mouth.

She'd dream again….. She drifted away.

~Arrival to the Hospital~

The patient and family advocate guided Duke to a check in area at the hospital and Duke gave them the information he knew about her. All he could do was wait. He sat in the waiting room chair, leaning forward with his head hanging down and arms resting on his thighs. He ran a hand through his hair and tried to think of the next task he needed to perform.

He called Rachel to tell her the news of Savanna being rescued alive. She was ecstatic but filled with deep worry for her cousin. "Duke—Oh my gosh! I cannot believe this has happened to her. We'll be there as soon as we can. Is she going to make it?"

Duke gave the best answer he could, "I hope so, Rachel. I think she might be ok, eventually," he said with hope in his voice.

"Well, Kate is dying to see you both, we're coming that way shortly. And Duke, thank you!"

Duke knew he had Bryan Bentley to thank for his assistance. He no longer felt conflicted about Cash's friend. Bryan redeemed himself and Duke decided to forgive him for betraying his brother.

~Chapter 39~

~The Hospital~

Rachel came out of Savanna's hospital room. "She didn't respond, but I think she can hear us. It's hard to fathom what that monster did to her. Duke, you look exhausted. Maybe you could go back to the hotel and shower—sleep for a while. I'll sit at her bedside in case she wakes up." She placed her hand on top of his.

"Thanks Rachel, but I'm not going anywhere until she's awake." He patted her hand.

"You're a good man, Duke Hollingsworth." She leaned her head on his shoulder for a second.

"Were you close to Savanna growing up," he asked, looking over at Rachel.

She nodded. "Savanna was the youngest of four. Her two oldest siblings were boys and then she had a sister just five years older than she was. Sam was the oldest, then there was Jaxon and then Jenna. Sam and Jenna were the family favorites. They could do no wrong. Savanna and Jaxon were the black sheep of the family. Jaxon took most of the physical abuse from their father, G.W. St. James. He was my dad's younger brother and was an angry man. But, Savanna was physically and verbally abused by both G.W. and her mother Elizabeth. To the outside world, their family was perfect, but Jaxon used alcohol and drugs to deal with the hell their parents dealt him at home. He and Savanna stuck together for support and he was really all she had until he committed suicide."

Rachel paused for a moment. "It crushed Savanna. She left home at eighteen before she had even graduated high school and then went to college to become a registered nurse. That's when she joined the military. I was the only one who knew about her brief marriage to Creed. My mother and father sided with her parents and always thought of her as an ill repute. They were never kind to her either. She's older than me, and I looked up to her as a big sister."

Rachel shook her head and looked pensive. "She's never really belonged anywhere…. not in her own family, not with Creed…. and not with her aunts and uncles."

Rachel looked over at Duke. "I think Kate and Cash were the first people to love her as she was. Cash apparently saw her as a jewel, because he gave her guardianship over Kate. Except for Brodie, he loved her too." Rachel smiled.

"She said that name one day when we were at the barn," Duke said. "Who was Brodie?"

Rachel sighed. "It's not really my story to tell, but I'm already knee deep in telling you Savanna's life story. Brodie was a yellow lab puppy that Creed bought her for Christmas when they first married. She loved that dog. In one of Creed's rages, Brodie tried to protect Savanna from him and he attacked Creed." She shuddered. "Creed shot him in the head right in front of her. She hasn't been able to entertain the thought of getting another dog since then."

Duke wished he'd known sooner. He might have understood her better and been able to help instead of blaming her for his brother's death and accusing her of being a gold-digger.

Guilt dug at his conscience. He had rejected her too, just like all the others. Not only had he rejected her, but he had enabled Ashley to put Savanna's life in danger.

He had to hand it to Savanna. She was tough as nails and determined—out on her own in the middle of nowhere—raising someone else's daughter. Meanwhile, other people were trying to give her a hard time and take away the only love she's ever known, with the exception of Rachel.

After all the crap-storms life had brought her, she was still kind. He rested his face in his hands. Exhaustion was claiming him, but his resolve to stay with Savanna, trumped anything else. For once, he wouldn't fail her. He'd stay by her side until he knew she was on the road to recovery.

~Chapter 40~

~The Awakening~

The morning light peeked through the blinds in the hospital room. Savanna opened her eyes to see the clock on the wall which said 6 a.m. She looked around the room for the first time. Flowers lined the room along with a get well banner. The door was closed, and the room was dimly lit with the morning light. She looked to her left and saw a man's loafer slippers and followed those feet up to a man's sleeping face. Duke was asleep at her bedside on a recliner bed with a thin blanket strewn haphazardly across his leg. Sleep tousled his hair. Outside the door, was the clatter of trays and meal-carts.

She couldn't remember how she got here. Duke stirred beside her and opened his eyes. She was looking at him as he awakened.

"You're awake," he said as he smiled and sat up, then came over to her bedside to hold her hand. He took her hand in his and covered it with his other. "How long have you been awake?" His voice held excitement.

She smiled back at him. "Just now," She whispered. Her voice had not yet recovered from being strangled by Creed.

"I am so glad you're awake. Are you in pain?" She shook her head.

"Where am I?" Her voice was at best a raspy whisper.

"Don't talk, something fractured your larynx, and it's trying to heal."

Duke took the next fifteen minutes giving brief explanations of what had happened in the last few days.

"What happened to Creed," she whispered.

Duke's dark blue eyes looked into hers. "He died from a gunshot wound. You shot him in self-defense."

Tears filled her eyes at all that had happened.

"I'm glad you're ok, Savanna. I'm so sorry for the way I treated you." He bent down and kissed her forehead.

She looked into his eyes and mouthed the words, "Thank you for saying that Duke. You're forgiven."

He told her how he had spoken with Bryan Bentley who had been close to Cash and that Cash knew she was a wonderful woman—a saint. Otherwise, he would have never left Kate with her.

He explained that his past fueled his disdain for her and that it was nothing of her own fault. All this new information left her reeling. His face looked as handsome as ever as he spoke to her and she felt lucky that he was at her bedside even if he didn't belong to her, but to Ashley. Savanna was wondering where Ashley was and if she knew that Duke had stayed the night at her bedside.

A nurse interrupted their conversation as she opened the door to do her morning rounds. "Ms. St. James, you're awake! That's great news. I'm going to do an assessment and get some vital signs. The doc should be around to see you shortly." Savanna smiled and interacted with the nurse as best she could with her voice gone.

Duke stepped out into the hall to call Kate and Rachel about Savanna's progress. He was eager to tell them the good news.

Abby's parents brought Kate to the hospital later that day and Duke had met them in the lobby to bring Kate up to Savanna's room.

She beamed with joy as she saw Kate's face coming through the door.

Kate made her way over to Savanna and leaned over to hug her. "Kate," she whispered and Kate clung to her for a moment then straightened and looked at her.

"You look better than you did a few days ago." She smiled down at Savanna. "I missed you so much."

Duke stood on the other side of her bed watching the exchange between the two. Gratitude filled him that the two people he cared about were safe and with him.

The next few days, Rachel visited and insisted that Savanna come home with her and Bear for a few days while she recovered. Savanna had a few follow-up appointments with a specialist for her laryngeal fracture and Rachel volunteered to transport her to and from them and Savanna didn't object.

The thought of her cousin caring about her well-being warmed her and the knowledge that Duke had stayed by her side after he had helped to rescue her from the boat, shocked her.

Duke took Kate home after he knew Savanna was ok and Rachel was looking after her.

~Chapter 41~

Over the next few days, she stayed with Rachel and Bear who made a fuss. She wasn't used to being such a spectacle. Savanna hadn't seen or heard from Duke or Kate since they discharged her from the hospital. Although, Kate face-timed her a few times. Communication was easier that way since she still had no voice.

Kate's sun-lightened hair and her bronzed skin were evidence of all the time spent outdoors at camp. Savanna asked her to tell a few camp stories. They laughed together about her experiences with camp food and her summer boyfriend, Shane.

Duke butted in on that part of the conversation to tell her that Shane better watch his step.

Kate rolled her eyes at her uncle and said "You're not supposed to be eavesdropping Uncle Duke! This is a girls-only conversation." She raised her voice in protest to his antagonism. He laughed and let them finish their face-time session. Savanna couldn't help but notice how handsome he looked behind Kate in the video.

"Hi Savanna." He waved at her and she waved back. His presence on the screen tugged at her heart. She wished she could thank Cash for bringing these two wonderful people into her life. She'd be forever thankful for the twist of fate that brought them together.

She couldn't deny that she had feelings for Duke any longer, she was in love with him. Savanna wanted him to be happy, even though Ashley had Duke's heart and his ring. She'd have to stamp out her feelings for him. Other than seeing him on that face-time call with Kate, he didn't seem to be in her life. It was only natural that he wouldn't be hanging around her since Ashley was in the picture.

She longed for things to be like they were before Creed Kelley disrupted her life. Maybe, just maybe, Duke would consider letting Kate live with her again, since the danger had passed and the courts no longer required that she stay away from Kate. She could at least ask, after she summoned up the courage. The worst that could happen is that he would say no.

Kate stayed with Rachel and Savanna while Duke and Bear drove to Hilton Head Island to retrieve her belongings and her car. The state completed the investigations on her case and had cleared her of any wrong-doing. She wondered if Ashley had accompanied them but she didn't ask, as no one had even mentioned her name.

She smiled with relief when she saw Bear and Duke pulling into the driveway in Duke's truck. They dropped her car off in her garage before making their way to Bear's house. "What a sweet thing to do." She thought and was in awe of their kindness.

Bear's tall frame entered the house, and he tossed off his ball cap and kissed Rachel on the lips. "Hey Rache, I missed you." The two embraced for what seemed like an eternity and Savanna couldn't help being a little envious. But, she was happy for them.

Duke snatched Kate's phone out of her hand to annoy her like an obnoxious sibling would do. "Give it back Uncle Duke!" She shouted as she jumped to reach the phone he had dangled high above her head. Her attempts to reach it were futile due to his height, so she tried to tickle him while he had his arm raised in a strategy to retrieve her phone. Although he was annoying her, she enjoyed the attention. Savanna watched them interact and smiled.

He gave Kate's phone back to her after several minutes of being a pest and then turned to Savanna. "Well, you're looking better every day."

She nodded as she still had no voice. The sight of him gave her butterflies and her mouth cracked another smile. The bruises on her throat faded and her face had returned to normal except for small discolorations on the temple. They removed the stitches in her forehead and the area was feeling less itchy.

Rachel looked at Savanna as Duke asked if they wanted to attend a fireworks display on the edge of town.

"Do you feel up to it," Rachel asked and Savanna nodded with excitement. Getting outdoors, and going back to normal, sounded like heaven.

Kate and Duke would meet them at the edge of town around 8 p.m. A meal of hot dogs, potato chips and watermelon were on the menu for the evening.

~Fireworks~

Tank top and shorts clad, Savanna pulled a small ice chest on rollers behind her, while Bear and Rachel carried lawn chairs and a blanket. The heat and humidity hung in the air, but the mood was still festive. Giddiness surged through her when she thought of fireworks since they were her favorite. The explosions around the 4th of July sometimes brought back memories of the night she sustained the scar down her left arm, but she had learned to conquer her fear. Tonight, being with people she loved, made all the difference.

She saw Kate running toward them across the green grass wearing a lawn-chair sack on her back. She was brimming with excitement and hugged them as she approached.

"Uncle Duke got delayed and will be here in a minute," she said with an eye roll.

There was no mention of Ashley and Savanna was wondering if she was even in town. "I'm—like—starving, can we get some food?" Kate whined.

Rachel chimed in, "Me too. Let's get our food and bring it back. Savanna, you can stay with our stuff and we'll get your food."

Savanna nodded as Bear, Rachel and Kate walked toward the food vendors.

She watched as the crowd grew and people were placing lawn chairs along with picnic blankets on the grassy knoll near them.

Momma Lynn came by and spoke with Savanna. "I'm so glad you're ok. I love that Duke thought to call me when he needed help with Kate. Duke is a good man. I'm thankful he brought you back to us."

Savanna shook her head in agreement and hugged Momma Lynn.

She saw Ellis Perkins and his wife who stopped to say hello. She wasn't able to speak to them and they understood as they had just stopped by to wish her well. Their kindness touched her.

Getting the food took a long time since the line had been long. Rachel and Bear had also stopped to talk to acquaintances along the way.

In the distance, Savanna saw a tall form and knew instantly that it was Duke. He was by a tree talking to…

Ashley? "I guess the battle ax is in town," she moaned to herself. The animation in Ashley's arm gestures looked serious. Ashley dropped her arms by her side as Duke spoke. The conversation went on for a few more minutes and then she kissed him on the mouth. A few people walked into Savanna's line of sight and blocked her view.

Kate and the others came back with arms full of food. Hot dogs, potato chips, little containers with cubed watermelon, pickles and bottled water. Savanna's mouth watered just smelling the juicy hot dog. The smell of the food made her forget about Duke and Ashley for a moment.

Rachel's phone rang, and she searched her bag to answer it. "Hello... Yeah, Kate's with us. We just got you some food." She listened to the voice on the other end. "Oh, I see. Yeah... it's no problem." Rachel sighed as she hung up. "Duke will join us a little later.... said he had some loose ends to tie up. Whatever that means." Rachel shrugged.

"Must be something to do with the horses," Kate said.

"*More like, something to do with a horse's behind.*" She smiled to herself at her malicious thought and was glad no one could read her mind.

The fireworks display was spectacular and Duke never showed up but had called to say that he would pick up Kate from Rachel's house. Rachel had convinced him to let her spend the night with them and he had agreed. Savanna's thoughts kept drifting back to the scene in the park with Ashley talking to Duke under the tree. She assumed they wanted alone time and went back to his house. Her unhappiness grew as she thought about it.

~Chapter 42~

Savanna was missing home and Rachel had taken her to a specialist appointment for her larynx. Her voice was coming back although it was still hoarse. She followed the doctor's instructions for healing.

"I appreciate everything you've done for me, Rache. Driving me around and speaking for me when I needed help. You're a great cousin to have around... ya know," she croaked out and Rachel laughed.

"I'm so glad I could help after all you've been through."

Savanna looked at her. "I thought since I'm much improved, I can return home to care for myself."

Rachel smiled. "You bet, cousin—we'll go by and get your things and take you out to your place." Savanna gave her a thumbs up as her voice was playing out at the moment.

It was dusk when Rachel brought her home, and Savanna unlocked the door. "Everything looks the same," she said as she walked through the house but stopped when she saw the back door. "What's this?" Surprise and confusion filled her when she saw that the back door was new and she opened it to inspect it.

"Yeah, Duke came by and replaced it for you before he and Bear went to South Carolina to get your car."

"Why—what happened," she whispered.

"Duke kicked in your screen door and back door looking for you on the day you left. He broke the glass and damaged the door during his frantic search."

Warmth filled her heart again as she thought about him being concerned for her and even bothering to find her. She blinked back tears as she thought about all he had done to save her life. She hugged Rachel and thanked her for her kindness and how much it had meant to her.

"Call me if you need anything—Sav." Savanna nodded and made a heart sign with her hands as Rachel walked out the door.

Fatigue set in and she prepared for bed and crawled under the covers to let sleep claim her. The sheets were cool and comfortable and while it was great being taken care of at Rachel's house, there was nothing like her own bed. She slept.

~Chapter 43~

Savanna brewed a cup of her favorite coffee and took it outside to the front porch just as the sun was peeking above the trees. The air was light and cool before the heat of the morning set in. With the first swig of coffee, the taste was rich, and the warmth felt divine on her throat. For the first time in a long time, she was happy. As the morning sun illuminated her property, she noticed multiple fence posts placed along the acreage. She almost choked to see that someone had also erected a new barbed wire fence.

Coffee sloshed on her bare feet as she rushed from her chair on the front porch, to the house, to slip her feet on some shoes, and scramble for the ATV keys. The ground rushed by as she made her way to the fence line. Someone had finished placing all her fence posts and strung the barbed wire. She covered her mouth with her hands. Who—Duke? It had to be him.

She wanted to call but wasn't sure her voice would hold up over the phone. "How sweet!" She wanted to thank him in person no matter if his battle ax of a fiancé was there. It was a big deal to her that he'd gone to so much trouble. She knew the work he had to have put in.

Savanna put on her make-up and pulled her hair into a ponytail. Shorts and a T-shirt were the outfit of the day. Temps were going to be warm. She grabbed her bag and headed out the door to Duke's place. To her relief, Ashley's car wasn't in the driveway.

She rang the doorbell a few times, but no one answered. Duke's truck sat outside the barn. The gravel crunched beneath her sneakers as she made her way around. The horses' whinny and the sound of hooves on the ground bustled in the barn.

Savanna walked through and saw Jesse in his stall. She gave him a rub on the face and with her raspy voice, talked to him in her usual baby talk.

"I thought we talked about this—he'll never learn to speak correctly if you keep using baby talk." Duke smiled at her.

She startled and smiled to see Duke standing a few feet from her. She hadn't heard him approach. "I can't resist," she said.

"Jesse and I are glad to see you, but what brings you all the way out here," he asked in a teasing tone.

Her hands dropped to her sides as she faced him. "I came out here to ask who might have finished my barbed wire fence," she croaked out.

He smiled a boyish smile which was charming, considering his size. He spread his arms out wide, "guilty."

Her laugh was soft and seemed to be the only sound in the barn. The world faded away as he looked at her.

"I don't even know what else to say, but thank you," she rasped. "Thank you doesn't seem to be enough."

He walked toward her while taking off his gloves. As if in slow motion, he pulled her toward him and held her in an embrace. She clung to him for a moment. While embraced in his arms, utopia claimed her. She wasn't sure how long they stood like that. He pulled back from her embrace and his eyes looked into hers. Nothing mattered to her in that moment as his mouth claimed hers. She would enjoy this moment for the rest of her life.

As he pulled away, the thought of Ashley permeated her mind, along with guilt.

"I'm sorry, I shouldn't ha—"Savanna whispered.

"Sorry for what?"

"You're engaged to Ashley and I'm here… in this barn, kissing her fiancé," she rasped out.

A smile breached his lips. "There is no Ashley, we called it quits before I looked for you in South Carolina."

Savanna's mouth gaped open. "Really? I saw you in the park at the fireworks display and she kissed you. I wasn't aware you weren't together then. What happened," she asked.

"Savanna—Ashley is the one who told Creed where you were in exchange for any salacious information on you that would help me get guardianship of Kate. When I found out and confronted her, she showed her true colors. I don't want that in my life, or around Kate." Savanna was relieved to know he had seen what kind of person his former fiancé was, but she was shocked to learn that Ashley had almost gotten Kate—and her, killed.

Savanna stood in silence for a moment as the news sank in.

"I felt so guilty that all this happened to you because of me, so I tried to avoid you as much as possible after you were discharged from the hospital. The guilt was the same as when I was injured in battle and had to leave my platoon behind. I just couldn't face you for a few days," he said.

Savanna shook her head at his words. "Duke, you saved my life. Even if Ashley hadn't been the one to tell Creed where I was, he would have eventually found me. Thank God, I had you looking out for me…. my personal hero." She smiled after she said it. "I'm so grateful for all you've done for me… fixed a faucet, fixed my doors, finished my fence, not to mention rescuing me off a boat in the middle of the Atlantic, when I was on death's door. You're a good man Duke Hollingsworth."

"Let's just say I'm a work in progress. When I was in battle in the Middle East, I came back wounded and also had to deal with losing my buddies in the war. Along with the guilt of leaving my platoon, I had lost my identity and my dignity. The woman whom I thought would be by my side, betrayed me. Her name was Calista, and she was a tall blonde—like you."

Savanna smiled but said nothing so that he would continue.

"I was very bitter toward women after that and thought they were all after money and status, but I especially had it in for tall blonde ones who reminded me of her."

"I wish I had known that months ago, I would have changed my hair color," she joked.

He rested his forehead on hers. "Savanna, I'm in love with you."

Jesse snorted in the background after Duke spoke. Savanna couldn't believe she had just heard Duke speak those words.

He loves me? Is this for real? She questioned herself. Her mouth opened in surprise.

"Do you know when I first knew I was in love with you?"

She smiled and shook her head, waiting for his answer. "Well… when I first laid eyes on you in Leland Owen's office, you took my breath away. I knew I was in trouble when I saw those blue-green eyes looking at me. But, when you stood up to me in the diner and told me how you'd exchanged favors with my brother and acted like it was none of my business, I was hooked."

"You were a mystery that I was hell bent on unraveling—the funny thing is—I'm the one who came unraveled. I couldn't stay away from you… I would drive to your house to visit Kate," he said with air-quotes, "because I needed an excuse to get near you."

"Ashley provided the barrier I needed to keep my wits about me." He kept his eyes on hers as he talked. "I hated women for a long time and Ashley was convenient because I didn't have to love her. She only wanted status and to use my SEAL history for future political purposes.

When I told Kate the reason I had taken over guardianship of her on the way home from camp, she was distraught, broken-hearted and begged me to help you. Her sorrow ripped my heart out. It took me until that moment to realize that you had been fighting on your own for a long time. I vowed to help you so you didn't fight alone. I'm sorry it took me so long to stop denying my feelings for you and figure it out. It never occurred to me that I was so bitter against the opposite sex until Kate—a teenager, had to beg me to help you."

Savanna sniffled at his explanations and wrapped her arms around him. It felt like home, as her head rested on his chest.

"I'm in love with you too, Duke Hollingsworth," she said as she hugged him.

He pulled away to look at her face. "For real? You love me?"

She nodded yes.

He took her face between his hands. "Do you know how happy I am right now?"

She wanted to say more, but she just nodded instead, for lack of voice. "I realized I had feelings for you when you brought Kate back at Christmas and I didn't have to be alone. I knew that she wouldn't have been able to come back if you hadn't been so kind as to bring her back to Georgia, and then you helped us prepare dinner and took care of my foot," she whispered then laughed. "I'm a walking disaster! One injury after the other. Maybe I'll wrap myself in bubble wrap," she said, and he raised his eyebrows.

"Hmm... tantalizing thought," he said as he smirked at her. "How about I stop sneaking up on you so you don't injure yourself?" She laughed and nodded in agreement.

~Chapter 44~

July passed, and the Georgia heat hounded them, but the summer had turned out to be the happiest of her life. She spent all her spare time with Kate and Duke when she wasn't working. Duke spent most of his evenings at her house, and Kate went back and forth between the two homes. She was thriving as she had a mom and dad figure in her life.

Momma Lynn came over to Savanna's place to show her how to preserve the peaches that had grown over the summer. The peach trees were heavy with fruit and they carried bushels into the house and began to peel them in an assembly line. Duke showed up one evening and began eating a juicy one. The peach juice was running off his chin and dropped to the floor and he'd somehow managed to track a peach in on his work boots. "Edward Duke Hollingsworth, you are tracking peaches all over this floor!

I just mopped it an hour ago—I'm gunna whoop yer butt! Wipe yer feet on the mat before you come in this kitchen, you hear?" Momma Lynn scolded him and Savanna laughed at him for getting in trouble.

"Yes, ma'am! I'll never let it happen again," he said as he walked over to Savanna and hugged her from behind. "What are you laughing at," he said to Savanna as she stood there with a paring knife and a peach in her hand.

Momma Lynn was special to them both, as a mother figure. Duke couldn't remember the last time he'd felt such happiness.

Duke, Kate and Savanna visited Glenn Oaks cemetery to leave fresh flowers at Cash and Amy's graves. Savanna's voice was recovering. "Isn't it something…Cash always wanted us to all meet in Georgia," she said as they looked across the cemetery lawn. A slight breeze was the only other sound as peace surrounded them.

Duke looked over at her, "I guess we did."

The three of them missed him, but were forging on with life. A few months prior, they had placed Amy's remains in Glenn Oaks beside Cash, just as he'd requested.

One evening, Kate spent the night with Abby, and Savanna went to Duke's to learn horseback riding. All went well, and she was bonding with the horse. She and Duke rode out in the lush green pasture. The day was perfect. The love in her heart for him only grew the more they spent time together.

As they rode back to the barn, Savanna dreaded her time with him to end. Every minute was magical. He helped her get her horse squared away after their ride. She thought he had gone to do one more thing and stopped to wait on him. When she turned around, he was on one knee. "Duke, what are you do—?" She covered her mouth in astonishment.

He was holding a diamond ring in a black velvet box toward her. "Savanna Katherine St. James, will you marry me?"

His proposal stunned her, and tears filled her eyes. "Yes! I will."

He stood and put the ring on her finger and sealed the deal with a kiss.

As if on cue, Jesse snorted in the background. "You make me so happy," he said as he held her in a tight embrace. She looked up at him.

"How did you know my middle name?"

He shook his head. "The day Leland spoke your whole name in that law office, it was seared in my mind from then on. Although in desperation, I tried to forget it, but God apparently wanted you in my life. Fate—isn't that what you called it when Cash crossed your path?"

"Yes, God's plan and fate brought us together," she said.

~Chapter 45~

Savanna spent the next few months wedding planning. Kate would be a bride's maid and Rachel would be her matron of honor. Bear agreed to walk her down the aisle. She wrestled with the fact that she'd have to invite her Uncle Phillip and Aunt Marcia who hated her, but she would invite them out of respect to Rachel, although she knew that Rachel would never insist that she did.

She and Duke tasted cakes and decided on the flavor of their wedding cake. He left the rest of the details to her.

"I think I'll go with roses for the bouquets," Savanna told Rachel.

"I thought pink Ranunculus were your favorite."

"I'm going to have a new favorite flower and it's not going to include pink Ranunculus." Savanna laughed.

"Hmm, I can't imagine why," Rachel said and smiled.

Duke laughed when she told him the story about Aunt Marcia accosting her at Rachel's wedding and how his brother had stepped up to save the day. "Sounds just like something he'd do…. able to make up a white lie on the spot. I miss him—wish he could be my best man,"

Savanna thought about Rachel's wedding when her Aunt Marcia commented on the fact that she was in her early forties and needed to *"Keep up the Botox or whatever it is you're doing."*

Savanna also remembered the snarky comment about there not being enough fish in the sea at her age, and how there were *"only puddles with icky tadpoles"* left for her. She forgave her Aunt for saying that, because only insecure and miserable people put others down. She'd learned that in her lifetime.

~The Rehearsal Dinner~

Laughter and fun filled the rehearsal dinner. Savanna announced to her guests while holding a microphone, "I've been told by some that this is peculiar, but at age 16, I wrote a letter to my future husband. I wrote this at a time when dreams and hope for receiving love was all I had. I kept it all these years and a few weeks ago pulled it out of a box. It's funny, because Duke checks the boxes on my wish list from decades ago and I'm going to read aloud to all of you tonight."

Family and friends found humor in the sentiment as the crowd erupted in laughter. She continued on after the place quieted down.

Duke watched her stand there and read it aloud. His face was red, but held a smile.

To my future husband:

I don't know your name or what color your eyes are, but I bet you'll be tall and a hero type of guy. I think you'll probably be handsome too. It's ok if you wear a baseball hat or a cowboy hat as long as you love me just the way I am." Savanna laughed and wiped the corner of her eye as she said those words. *"I don't know when our paths will cross, but I do know that I've been waiting for you my entire life. By the time you meet me, I'll be everything you want and need, and you'll be everything I asked God for. I have already thanked Him for you in advance, and I love you already.—Love Savanna*

P.S. I hope you love animals too.

She looked up from her letter at him and said, "So Duke, even as much as I love you at this moment, I loved you even back then."

Applause came from her guests along with "Aww." A few people were wiping their eyes when she finished.

She sat down by Duke who gave her a hug and kiss.

~Their Wedding Day~

She gazed in the mirror at her reflection. Today, she didn't have to cover the scar on her left arm with make-up. The sheer lace sleeve overlay which covered the deep V-neck bodice, hid the scar.

Rachel straightened Savanna's dress behind her. This dress—it was everything she could have ever dreamed of.

"Wow, it's very similar to Kate Middleton's dress," Rachel remarked with humor.

"That's what I was going for, Rachel," Savanna teased.

"It's too bad your Mee Mee Jane isn't alive to attend your wedding. I bet she would have bought you some pretty white *pain-iz* for your bridal shower. I hear they cost *good money*." Kate held a straight face as she said it.

Rachel busted up laughing and asked, "You told Kate about Mee Mee Jane's panties?"

"I did!" Savanna was trying to contain her laughter.

"I told her what we did to Mee Mee Jane—May she rest in peace." Savanna said.

"Kate Hollingsworth, you are too funny!" Rachel hugged a grinning Kate.

As Kate and Rachel had stepped out into another room to gather their bouquets, there was a knock at the door. Bryan Bentley stood there holding an envelope. She drew in a breath as she saw him. The last time she took an envelope from him was the day he delivered the news about Cash's death.

His face wore a reassuring smile. "Savanna, this time, it is good news, I promise—and you make a beautiful bride."

She took the envelope from his hand. "Bryan, I can never thank you enough for helping Duke find me. Your actions saved my life. Thank you for being a friend to Cash and now Duke. I never got to tell you that since I made it home."

He looked at her and winked. "I'm glad I could be of help to you. From what Cash told me, you deserve all the happiness." She hugged him and he walked away as she shut the door. Her hands shook as she opened the envelope.

Dear Savanna,

I bet you never thought you would marry me, of all people, when you met my brother in Germany all those years ago. I bet you never guessed when you saw me on the day of the reading of his will, that we'd be in this place today with all the people we love surrounding us, and watching us exchange our vows.

I thought I would never love again, and then you walked into my life. I don't know what I've done so right that I'd deserve someone like you.

Who would have thought that two people in their forties would end up together without kids of their own, but gaining a daughter? I can't think of anyone else more perfect for sharing my life with. If I could pick the perfect prototype for my wife and the person who will be a mother to Kate, it would be you. I can't wait to spend my life with you. I'll be waiting for you at the altar in my tux, but without my cowboy hat.
Love,
Duke

The note made her laugh and cry. Taking care not to ruin her makeup, she dabbed her eyes with a tissue.

She loved him more than words could say as she'd always wondered if anyone would ever love her just as she was.

Bear knocked on her door. "It's time Savanna, you ready?"

She folded the letter. "I'm ready," she said as she opened the door and walked down the corridor with her arm linked through his.

"Duke's a lucky man today," he said as he walked with her. He chuckled as they walked.

"What are *you* laughing at?" She looked at him sideways.

"I was just hoping that today you don't lose a shoe like you did on New Year's Eve," he joked. Her hand tightened on his arm playfully.

"I'll try not to lose my shoe today… Sugar Bear."

He looked confused. "Sugar Bear?"

Just before they opened the door to the sanctuary, she explained how she'd laughed at the name *Bear* when she first read his wedding invitation, and thought up ways they had probably teased him as a kid. Sugar Bear was one of them.

"I'm glad Duke's marrying you today instead of me.... you're a handful." He grinned, and she enjoyed their private joke together. "For the record, and because you brought it up, they called me *Pooh Bear* since I'm so adorable."

She laughed as the door to the sanctuary opened. "Let's do this," she said, and they started down the aisle.

Standing tall on the hill at the edge of town was the First Presbyterian Church, a beautiful large refurbished white landmark. Three hundred people who loved Savanna and Duke filled the place.

Duke looked dashing standing at the altar waiting for her in his tuxedo. Bear was walking her down the aisle. Kate and Rachel had preceded them and were standing at the front of the church in black gowns with deep burgundy and pink rose bouquets.

The orchestra played the wedding march. She could see Duke looking at her as she walked toward him. His eyes held nothing but love for her. She could feel his love and the love of Rachel and Kate who would also stand beside her in a moment.

The energy in that church was nothing but love. She saw Momma Lynn smiling at her and dabbing her eye with a handkerchief and Ellis Perkins on the next row. She even glanced at her Uncle Phillip and Aunt Marcia as she walked, but instead of resenting them, she wished them well.

Savanna thanked God for this moment…. this feeling… it was unlike anything she'd ever known. Then it occurred to her… it's because at last, she found where she belongs.

~*The End*~

Made in the USA
Monee, IL
07 September 2023